I0685496

Published by Lift Bridge Publishing

Copyright © 2014 by Carolyn T. Brookman

All Rights Reserved

Library of Congress Cataloging-in-Publication Data

Brookman, Carolyn T.

The Black Pelican

Book Cover artist: Lily Claire Brookman

ISBN 978-0-692-24012-0

PRINTED IN THE UNITED STATES OF AMERICA

FIRST EDITION

Did you ever feel that you were at the right place, at the right time, and did you ever while at that place have unusual feelings of peace and total happiness? Well, these are things that Catharine and her mother and father found when they relocated to The Outer Banks of North Carolina from London. Catharine's father was a very privileged man whose father was very wealthy, but never spent much time with his family because he was too busy making money. Her father wanted something different for his own family and decided to relocate the family to America, where he would make his own way in the world. So their lives of luxury were no more to be.

However, as they neared the Carolina coast a violent Nor'easter bore down on them. They were in horrific danger and but for the braveness of The Black Pelican, whose courage is well known in the Outer Banks, they would have been lost. Legend has it that he alerted lifesaving station crews when ships were in danger by swooping down again and again until they followed him to the vessel in trouble.

But when Catharine returned to England because of a family illness, she realized that what she treasured most in her life had changed. She became so homesick for the things she had grown to love - the simple beauty of a sunrise or sunset, walking barefoot on the beach looking for shells and seaglass, a gathering of friends and neighbors to share food, laughter, dancing and singing and, most importantly, a young man named Seth - these were the important things to her now.

Little did she know that while in London she had spoken with such love and yearning about this new home of hers that when at last she was able to return home she would bring a boatload of new "Bankers" with her!

Nor did she know that out there was a brave, black bird keeping a watchful eye!

THE BLACK PELICAN

By Carolyn T. Brookman

THE BELOVED BLACK PELICAN

The evening was dark and storm clouds rolled.
Winds blew and howled as rain beat and poured.

But one look skyward as that dark storm did blow,
Caused fears to subside, gave hearts new hope.

A magnificent bird, renowned for his valor,
Would gallantly, fearlessly lead them ashore.

C. T. Brookman

THE CAST OF CHARACTERS

Catharine Chase - Young English Lady now residing in the Outer Banks

Thomas, III and Elizabeth Chase - Catharine's Father and Mother

Thomas Chase, II - Catharine's Grandfather

Seth Winters - Young Man born and raised on the Outer Banks

John and Martha Winters - Seth's Mother and Father

Sarah - John & Martha Winters' Daughter

Abe - Sarah's Husband

Anna Catharine - Sarah & Abe's Infant Daughter

Jake Parks - Wealthy Man-About-Town and Grandfather's Assistant

Father Sam - Beloved Priest of the Outer Banks

Mrs. King - Grandfather's Nurse

Mr. Spencer - Grandfather's Old Friend and Former Business Colleague

Detective Casey - Scotland Yard Detective

William - Grandfather's Butler

Molly - Catharine's Best Friend

Patrick Kelly - Grandfather's Doctor and Close Friend

THE BLACK PELICAN

PART ONE

CHAPTER ONE

The Outer Banks of North Carolina
May, 1901

The warm spring day caused Catharine's spirits to soar. The sky was an unmatchable North Carolina blue and the waves of the Atlantic Ocean lapped lazily close to her bare feet as she strolled on the shore. Sea Gulls laughed happily around her and pelicans sailed effortlessly overhead. As Catharine studied the pelicans her sight at once fell on the graceful, beautiful, Black Pelican who, obviously, was their leader and who held a beloved place in the hearts of all Outer Banks seamen.

Catharine knew from experience the courage and the braveness of this Black Pelican. He had swooped down relentlessly on the lifesaving station at Kitty Hawk during a violent Nor'easter until the Station Number Six lifesaving crew realized he was trying to get their attention and to tell them something. Their curiosity led them to follow the Pelican out into the fierce storm, and what they found was a vessel in serious trouble. Catharine knew first-hand of this courageous bird because she and her mother and father, Elizabeth and Thomas Chase, were among those on this boat. The Black Pelican was honored here, and when he swooped down to get the attention of the seamen at Station Number Six, his message was sure and certain. They knew somewhere nearby someone was in danger and needed their help.

Catharine's father, Thomas, who had been a wealthy businessman in London, had always dreamed of a new life in America. He was captivated with the idea of beginning a new venture of his own that he, himself, would found. Thomas had inherited his wealth, for which he was thankful, but he had always walked in the ever-present footsteps of his father who had undisputed authority in family business decisions. He felt it would be so satisfying if he, Thomas Chase, could begin over again and make use of the many ideas of his own that had never been put to use.

He knew that America was the place for this new start for him and his family. He had been so enthusiastic when talking about this dream that his wife and daughter also soon started wondering with interest about the journey from England to America. They also came to feel it could be a life-changing adventure, so much so that they too joined in on the dream and the exciting possibilities of this new life!

And succeed he did. First, in his new homeland, he opened a general store. Thomas brought with him from London many ideas new to the "Bankers" (a name used when speaking of the locals).

He built his "Chase Mercantile Company" with a certain swagger not before seen here. It would be pleasing to the eye with a certain section catering to the ladies only. There were toiletries and undergarments, there were dress patterns and fabrics, there were all sorts of sewing necessities... Just the kind of thing the women loved to browse through. And because all of the ladies were not overly handy with the needle and thread he enlisted the help of a talented seamstress, Molly, who in time also became Catharine's best friend on the island. Molly made dresses and any other articles of clothing the local ladies requested, and her work didn't go unnoticed by visitors and vacationers either. This caught on so well that soon he had to hire a second. So on it grew....

In another section of his store he sold only items that would interest men, such as sporting and fishing goods, men's clothing and tools. In another section he sold only foodstuff and household goods. He had opened the first department store in the Outer Banks without even realizing it, and it was a huge success!

When merchant ships sailed into port to trade, he and his workers were right there to check out the latest things and to purchase them for his customers. And now with the tourist trade growing by leaps and bounds, these new clients were coming in ever-increasing numbers, making it necessary to order merchandise in larger quantities and to enlarge his store regularly.

Catharine's mother, Elizabeth, had also lived her entire life in London until their move here. Of all of them, she probably had the most drastic life-style changes with which to adjust.

She was raised from birth also in a very privileged home and until making this move she had truly been pampered all of her life. Known throughout London for her beauty, stylish gowns, hair styles, parties, one of the most extravagantly furnished homes in London, and on and on goes the list.

So it was Elizabeth who was the hardest to convince that this move would work in their favor. In fact, at first there were, unbeknownst to Catharine, verbal disagreements between Elizabeth and Thomas. In the end though, when she realized how much this mattered to Thomas and Catharine, she agreed, though if the truth be known, not wholeheartedly, to the move. And you have to give her credit for the spirit she displayed regarding the loss of her life of privilege and pampering, because, of them all, Elizabeth's loss was most drastic. She truly enjoyed her life as it was. It was harder for her to understand giving up their grand home and, as she saw it, blessings, for some primitive land with not a sign of proper living, no maids, butlers, cooks....

It just didn't make any sense to her as it seemed to her that they already had the lifestyle of most people's dreams. And on top of that, they were leaving Grandfather Chase behind! She loved Grandfather Chase! Didn't any of this matter to them? Again, it didn't make a bit of sense to her! However, she loved her husband, and Catharine was without question the most precious thing in her life. And, just to further prove her to be the great lady that she is, she made up her mind that she would not be the cause of the ruination of their dream.

Even after their arrival as new residents of the Outer Banks, she still was known there for her beauty and sense of style. She never presented herself as being too grand but she was just accepted as wealthy and beautiful and stylish and everyone respected her for her graceful way. In fact, Thomas and Catharine both felt the same way. They were extremely proud of her ladylike charm and the way she handled the huge change in her life. Could it be said that maybe she enjoyed the elite position in which she found herself? You know, that could be so. But, anyway, she charmed these "Bankers" and maybe that was just what they needed!

At the age of eighteen, Catharine was a lovely and lively young lady. She had been educated in the best schools, and raised with all the privileges available to a family who had always known great wealth.

An only child, it was never known to her why she had no siblings, but she always knew in her heart that it was not that her mother and father did not want more children because they had loved her so unconditionally and completely for her entire life. Catharine had returned this love to them in so many ways that they were very content with their very special one-and-only daughter. They may not ever have other children, but Catharine brought such joy to them that they felt they already had experienced a fulfillment that some people with much larger families never knew.

This was a favorite pastime for her, strolling on the beach, letting her mind wander wherever it dared to go. There was absolutely no place on earth that she wanted to be but here.

What had been a life of privilege in London had surely changed greatly since their move to this quiet island. There were none of the comforts here that had been hers for the taking before their long journey across the sea. No grand parties that young ladies of her station were accustomed to hosting and attending. No grand gowns made especially for her and to wear solely for that one-time occasion. There were no wealthy, titled and handsome young men who constantly competed for her heart. Here there was only one of interest to her, so very different from all the young men she had known.

And Seth Winters hadn't the vaguest idea that Catharine ever even thought about him....

Seth was a twenty-two year old young man who had grown up under the tutelage of his father, John Winters, to be an expert seaman, boat-builder and the ever-present and vigilant Keeper of Lifesaving Station Six at Kitty Hawk. Seth was blonde and handsome, however, he had no idea of this. These things were of no importance to this busy and talented young man.

His father, John, had relinquished the important responsibility as Keeper of Lifesaving Station Six to Seth when he reached his twenty-first birthday. John was so happy that his only son had chosen to follow in his footsteps, and he was also ready to have more free time to devote to his deepest passion which was boat-building, and leave the more strenuous lifesaving duties to Seth.

John was sixty years old now and did not have the strength or endurance needed for fighting to save lives being threatened by nor'easters or hurricanes in the Outer Banks. He would just leave that to the younger men and enjoy his boat building, and possibly enjoy some leisure time to just piddle! Yes, he would like that.

John Winters had lived in the same cottage near the ocean all of his life. He learned boat-building and seamanship from his father, who taught John everything he knew about the art of boat-building and John, in turn, passed it down to Seth. However, John could tell that Seth was going to be the most talented boat-builder of the three of them. People from miles away came to order boats to suit their needs from John Winters & Son. In fact, even now, Seth was in contact with a boat-builder from England who was interested in techniques used by John Winters and Son that currently weren't being used by his company in London. And, on the other hand, Seth was interested in learning about certain techniques currently being used in the London shipbuilding company that John Winters & Son had not as yet used and which Seth believed might be used to their own advantage.

Martha Winters, Seth's mom, was a small, hard-working woman who made every hour of her day count. She was much loved in the "Banks" because of her constant awareness of the needs of them all. Almost daily there was a meal being prepared by Martha for one of her neighbors who for one reason or another was in need of a gesture of neighborly love. While she made lunch for her husband and Seth she usually had a pot on cooking for one of them that Seth and his dad would deliver on their way back from lunch. Martha could be depended on to lighten someone in need's load and "Bankers" never forget these acts of kindness nor the giver of them.

All areas of keeping a home were hard work here in Coastal North Carolina at the turn of the century with very little time for luxuries like walking and sitting by the sea. But do you know that she found the time to do just that. Martha would hurry to get housework done every day so she could have that hour to herself to meditate and reflect on her life.

She was thankful for her life. She felt blessed to have a caring husband, her son, Seth, a daughter, Sarah, and her husband, Abe, who were expecting their first child soon. The excitement was building in this little family because this would be Martha and John's first grandchild.

Maybe it was because she felt so blessed that she felt she must be a blessing to someone else? It would be just like Martha to feel that way...

These happy thoughts and many others went through Martha's mind as she gathered sea glass, beautiful shells and momentums while moseying along the shore. The beauty that surrounded her every day never stopped amazing her and she thought, you know, this beauty is here for everyone. Not for just a few wealthy vacationers who were coming to the island in ever-increasing numbers, but this beauty is here free for the taking for everyone! This thought brought Martha a peaceful feeling and great happiness.

Their home was near the lifesaving station which made it easy for Seth and John to come home for lunch or to leave when there was an emergency at the station. On this particular day, Seth and John were talking excitedly as they neared the kitchen door at lunchtime. Martha laughed, "Goodness Gracious, What are you two up to today!" Seth replied that they all had been invited to a beach party and bonfire on Saturday night hosted by the Chase family. There will be a potluck supper and desserts would be appreciated too. Mr. Chase plays a mean fiddle, and so there may be some dancing too.

"What do you say, Mama?"

"Well," says Martha, "Of Course! We haven't had a good get together with the locals for a while."

"I'll have to check my canned goods and see what goodies I can come up with." Martha's thoughts were immediately occupied with recipes and such for the rest of the week.

"They like my blackberry cobbler and maybe I could also make chicken potpie.... I am so excited." Mentally she was already making plans as she thought "Good things always happen when neighbors get together!"

Seth thought to himself.... It would be a really good thing if

Catharine would notice that I am alive even! But she is so beautiful and well educated and used to things that I could never give her....

The week that followed was filled with a buzzing the likes not seen every day in these Outer Banks. Men gathered firewood for what would be a huge bonfire. Also, their responsibility was to provide tables for the delicious food the ladies would heap upon them, and benches so the older ladies and gentlemen could just sit, relax and be entertained and pampered. Men, women and children alike all loved their older folks and it brought them pleasure when they were allowed to do some small favor for them. So this small group was much celebrated and waited on at festivities like this.

Everyone would enjoy food, family, local news, reminiscing, a fair amount of folklore, watching the children play, and just reveling in the sights and sounds of a beautiful May evening.

Most guests at the party would sit on blankets spread out on the sand and the children would never sit down long enough to even worry about where they would sit!

The ladies scurried around gathering ingredients needed for their pies, cakes, side dishes.... The list never ended!

And Thomas Chase down at Chase Mercantile vowed he would run out of sugar, flour, butter, milk, chocolate, vanilla, lemon extract and the likes long before the party on Saturday night. But Thomas Chase's goods lasted.

He decided that one of Elizabeth's parties was definitely good for the economy! At last, the women's lists were filled and the cooking was done to perfection, and now....

CHAPTER TWO

(The Beach Party)

The party has begun! The food is appearing like magic! Benches and tables are set up and children are frolicking by the ocean. The water of the Atlantic is still a bit cool but they are finding many other ways to take advantage of this special time of freedom, fun, and the expectations of the long summer days which are close at hand.

Even Sarah and Abe, Seth's sister and her husband, are here. Sarah is getting much attention and is being escorted immediately to the seats reserved for the older guests, but with their baby due next month, nobody is taking the chance of Sarah getting overtired. They are just so happy that she and Abe are there and they want her just to sit back and enjoy the festive evening. And at this stage in her pregnancy, Sarah is most happy to do just that!

Also, among the guests coming in is Father Sam. He has a special place in the hearts and lives of everyone here for one reason or another. Father Sam was there when many of them were born, during their sicknesses, and during times of sorrow and death. But today, he is here to celebrate and enjoy his parishioners and friends. They are his family. He is theirs.

"Father Sam," Thomas Chase calls out, "Come on over here with us and have a touch of Kill Devil Rum!" Father Sam thinks to himself, "Am I up to this?" You see, the story goes that Kill Devil Rum got its name from the pirates who were no strangers to this island. They introduced the rum here and it was said to have been so potent and breathtaking that it would kill the devil! But on he goes to join in the revelry anyway.

While the men are enjoying their rum and telling tall tales, the ladies are putting the final touches on the food table. Meats, vegetables, side dishes, and desserts, each had their own section. Finally they have everything arranged to their liking and Elizabeth Chase asks Father Sam to bless the food, which gets a roar of approval from everyone.

Let the feasting begin! These ladies had prepared this feast from recipes, some of which had been passed down in their families for many generations, and only the favorite ones were prepared for this special table. The very special older guests went first. The children followed, with their mother's help. And, finally, the starving men's time came to fill their plates to the brim. After everyone else had settled down with their delicious meals, the Ladies filled their plates, telling each other how delicious their dishes were and asking them to share their recipes. The compliments were heard from everyone... "This is the best chicken I ever ate", "The seafood chowder is out of this world", and on and on they went, and ended with desserts that were so over-the-top that the moaning could be heard from every corner from a very happy and contented gathering of friends and neighbors.

Now the bonfire would be lit. The chill would be in the air shortly and everyone knew this and had brought coats and blankets to wrap up in while they sat around the fire. And soon the tale-telling would begin. Some of these same tales had been told around bonfires in the Outer Banks for many generations.

They told of long ago settlers and how each in their own way had changed the Banks. They told of pirates. Tales of Edward Teach, better known as Blackbeard, were favored locally because he used these islands as his home base. He was known far and wide for his pirating, but do you know, some sung his praises for acts of compassion that were also credited to his name and fame. The "Bankers" had bought his stolen goods because he offered trinkets and things they longed to have, and they were less expensive than British goods. His pirate era only lasted about two years, but it seems that even now, every time people gather to spin tales, yet another new and never before heard Blackbeard chapter has been added!

They loved telling how Nags Head got its name, how the "Old Nag", whose nightly prowlings on the shore with a lantern around his neck, lured ships too close to the shore, into the sand bars and their ships were then met with looters. Some local pirates made a living scavenging these ships for household goods, coins, jewelry and other valuables. And there was a bounty of valuable things aboard these vessels because many travelers brought their most precious possessions with them, as more than a few of these adventurers were planning on putting down roots here and never returning to their former homes.

While the stories rolled on, Catharine decided to walk down by the shore. The night was warm and moonlit. All the stars seemed to come out for the festivities too. Seth, who had been keeping a mindful eye on Catharine, pulled together all of his courage and, very discreetly, Seth found himself walking in that same direction.

"Hey Catharine, I am sure glad your folks came up with the idea to have this party. I never ate so much in my entire life, the food was delicious. Do you like to cook?" Seth thinks to himself, "Whoa, I am just rattling on! I need to give her a little chance to talk here"... But do you know that Shy Seth found that he had no trouble talking with Catharine at all! She told him that she would not be her mother's daughter if she didn't love to cook, "In fact," she said, "I made the blackberry cobbler, and I noticed that you had a second helping!"

They talked on and on. He told her of his adventures at the Lifesaving Station, some involving the bravery of the beloved Black Pelican, who was miraculously present in times of trouble. He told of how he loved building boats and what pride he felt each time he finished one and how satisfying it was to try to complete each one as close to perfect as he knew how.

He talked of his family and how they all were so happy to be having a new baby in the family soon and how Sarah and Abe stayed so busy getting things ready for him, or her! He said Sarah was sewing baby garments every spare minute and Abe was busy creating a nursery space and had just finished making the baby's crib. He said his mother, Martha, still had his and Sarah's crib that they had slept in, but they had decided to let it remain at Martha's and John's house so the new baby would have a napping space when they came to visit, which they all hoped would be really often!

Catherine told Seth about her life in London before she and her family started their great adventure. He asked her to tell him about how different life was there for her.

She told him that her father, Thomas, was a merchant in London. His father before him had been a successful merchant also, but he had always been so very involved in his businesses that he hadn't had much time to devote to Thomas. Thomas had always wished things could have been different between his father and himself. While he loved his father and his mother dearly, he had said when he was very young that when he had a family of his own, he would make sure that he was involved in their lives and that they would be involved in his. And he had! He had done the unthinkable by teaching his "daughter" about his and his father's businesses. He had thought his father would adamantly object to this, but to his amazement, his father did not. Thomas knew his father was devoted to Catharine and he sometimes felt that as his father aged, he was beginning to realize the value of his family, along with the value of his businesses and maybe, just maybe, even prioritizing a little.

Catharine's grandfather, she told him, was getting older now. She loved and missed him a lot and wondered if she would ever see him again. He wrote often and told her how he missed her. She was always so happy when the mail boat came with one of his letters.

She told Seth that her grandmother had been dead for some years now and that her grandfather lived alone with his servants who had been with him for many years. She, Thomas, and Elizabeth were his only close living relatives now and she knew he felt very alone and lonely.

This one thing made her feel sad when leaving London behind. Seth felt a sadness for Catharine as she spoke of her grandfather. He hoped that somehow she would one day be able to see him again. Then she possibly would feel happier when she thought of leaving him alone in London....

They talked about themselves and passions they both had in each of their lives. Seth spoke often about his love for building his boats and that the business was growing so fast he was going to have to make a decision soon about how he was going to be able to manage the ever growing boat building business and the lifesaving station.

Since his father had retired, he now led the crews at the lifesaving station also. Making a choice between them was going to be hard, but he felt it was one that would soon have to be faced. He told her of his adventures at the lifesaving station and how its crew's acts of bravery had saved so many lives over the years. The thoughts of giving up the lifesaving station were hurtful to him because that too was a part of him.

And, as before, they talked at length about the legacy of the legendary "Black Pelican".

Catharine had always loved playing her piano and she talked about playing for special events when she lived in London and how she had even loved to practice when she was a child. Seth himself knew first hand of Catharine's talent as she was always asked to play whenever there was an event where a piano was present. She now taught piano to the young people here, mostly girls, but she was pleased that two of her young male students were very talented. She played the piano in church on Sunday and for other special events. Father Sam who was a dear pastor and friend to everyone on the island felt she was heaven-sent to their little congregation because her music added an important dimension to their services.

But right now they could hear the fiddle tuning up and they knew a new round of the party was about to begin!

They headed back to be a part of the growing frenzy of clapping, singing and dancing too! Even the oldest of the guests were on their feet, though probably only for a short while, dancing and swinging to the fiddling and singing. Everybody there knew every song and dance that was played. After all, they had been hearing them all of their lives, and because they were all so familiar, it was so much the more special.

Not a person here was shy. They were all hooting and singing and dancing. Enjoying a night of happiness, under the full moon, by the beautiful sea, listening to the sounds of the waves lapping on the shore of the Atlantic, and hearing the happy sounds of music and laughter!

After a while, though, little ones started to droop, older ones started to yawn. Even the fiddle player, Mr. Chase, Catharine's father, was showing signs of fatigue. And shortly, one-by-one, each family thanked their hosts and told them what a memorable night it had been. They all told each other there had never been a meal as delicious as this one and slowly, but happily, made their way back to their homes.

The "Bankers" would have a quiet day tomorrow and rest. But they would talk for a long time about that grand night, and the night they first saw signs of romance blossoming....

CHAPTER THREE

(The Letter)

As usual, when Catharine saw the letter, which she immediately knew was from her grandfather, Thomas Chase, she was excited. Her grandfather always wrote of newsworthy tidbits that he knew would be of special interest to her like who was getting married, who was having a baby, who was having a party, and the likes. But as she opened and started to read this particular letter, she knew it was different from the others.

"My Dearest Catharine" it started, as he started all of his letters.

"I always love to write to you because mostly I have to remember all of the happy news since I last wrote to you, and this always leaves me smiling. However, this is not one of those times. This is a hard letter to write because I will be asking you to do something which may be a great inconvenience and burden to you, something I have never wanted to be." Catharine at once knew something was not right here....

"My doctors have told me that I may not have long to live. As you know, I am getting older now, but I have lived a long and rewarding life. Your father, mother and you have always brought such joy to my life. I only wish I had realized when I was younger how much of that I sacrificed in the name of fortune-building."

"Now I come to the hard part of this letter. I would like for you to make a journey to London to visit me. My fondest desire is to spend my final days with my dear Catharine and to hear your voice. I know this is a selfish thing that I ask, but it is the most important thing in the world to me."

"I want you to know that I have named you as the sole beneficiary of my estate, which you know is rather large. All of this has been settled with my legal advisors and requires no action on your part, however, there are many things I would like to talk over with you face-to-face. You will have all of my legal staff available to you as of today, so do not let this news bring you distress. My wish is that you will allow these things to bring you and those you love great pleasure."

"I mistakenly worked only to increase my fortune and did not enjoy the daily basic joys it could have brought to my life and the life of my family. My hope is that you will not make this same mistake. I have seen your keen business mind and I trust your wisdom and decision-making."

"Young Lady, you are now very wealthy, with the opportunity that few women have. What you decide to do with all this will be decided in the future, but I have no doubt at all that it will make me proud!"

"I will anxiously await your reply."

And he signed it.

"Your Loving Grandfather."

THE BLACK PELICAN

PART II

CHAPTER FOUR

(The Winds of Change)

Catharine was stunned. Her heart was racing and breaking at the same time. Her grandfather, who was the one reason she so hated to leave London, was dying. Oh, how she wished she weren't so far away from him. How she would love to be able to, right now, hold him in her arms, tell him how much she loved him and missed him.

She sat for a while looking out over the sea and cried for her grandfather. Catharine cried for her mother, father, and also she cried for herself. This letter would most assuredly bring changes to their quiet lives because there would be life-altering decisions that would have to be made. It made her head spin with all the confusing thoughts coming at her so furiously. She started to run home as fast as she could to let her father and mother know of this terrible news. "Oh," she thought, "I am so sorry to have to tell them," but did she have a choice? No.

Her father and mother were so very sad when they learned that Grandfather Chase's health had taken a turn for the worse. In fact, her father said that in recent letters his dad had told him how well he was getting along and how good he always felt about his father's uplifting letters.

His father had also told him though, that he had hired a young gentleman to help him handle his record keeping and book-keeping and the like because he didn't always feel up to dealing with their many complications. He said he knew that those things had to be handled just right and that sometimes he just didn't have the energy to deal with them. Thinking back on this though, it was certainly a big concession for his father to give up any area of control regarding his business, not even a small bit of control. That had always been against his very nature. But that line of thought hadn't occurred to him until now. He had figured his father was just finally ready to hand the some of the responsibility and head-aches over to others and take a much deserved and needed rest!

Catharine's mother fixed them all cups of tea, which always seemed to make any situation better. She was such a strong and supportive person and she insisted that her father-in-law had always been there for all of them. Even when Thomas decided to pursue a new life and career in America, Mr. Chase had not discouraged them. He had insisted that he was sure Thomas was headed in the right direction for himself and his family, and as he always said, he again said, that he was so proud of him. Catharine's mother was right, but Grandfather Chase was beginning to realize that his massive fortune was not the most important thing in the world to him. The most important thing in the world to him was his family, and they were not even on the same continent anymore!

That night was filled with the recalling of memories, with tears, and yes, even some laughter. But in the end, the discussion always came back to the request her grandfather had made asking for Catharine to come to London to visit him, and also to receive her inheritance. She wasn't sure how her mother and father would receive the request for this trip. But as they talked on into the night, they all knew that they could not deny this wish. He had consistently loved and cared for them and they had missed him daily, and they knew that he missed them probably even more.

So, the decision was made that night for Catharine to start preparations for the trip. There was much that had to be done and they knew they had to move quickly because they didn't know how much time they would have. They only knew that Catharine's passage should be booked on the next available ship to England. Catharine's father penned a letter to his father that night. Though it was late and they were all exhausted from the stress and long hours of decision-making, he knew this was something that he wanted to do right now. Waiting until the morning would not be acceptable because Thomas felt an extreme urgency within. He knew his father well enough to know that it wasn't part of his character to be overly excited in his decisions or to jump prematurely to conclusions of any kind, much less one of this caliber.

CHAPTER FIVE

(Preparing for the Journey)

And so it began. Thomas' letter to his father told him that Catharine would be arriving in London as soon as suitable accommodations could be made for her trip. He told his father how much he loved him and how he appreciated his unconditional love his entire life and the discipline that he instilled in him all of his life. He told him how he wished he were here with them because there was so much here he would like to show him and there were so many questions he would like to ask him, so much advice he still needed from him.

And let me tell you that later when Grandfather Chase read that letter his heart was overjoyed. There is nothing, Grandfather Chase reflected, more rewarding in life than to be loved and needed by those you love. After re-reading his letter and re-reading it again, Thomas finally decided it was ready to make the long journey to London. But he did tell Grandfather Chase that he would write again as soon as final passage for Catharine had been booked, letting him know her estimated date of arrival and any other information he might need.

The next week was akin to a beehive at the Chase household. Catharine would need to have suitable clothes for her journey and the seamstresses were engaged right away. Fortunately, Molly, one of the seamstresses and Catharine's best friend, waited for each shipment from England which would bring her sketches of the latest fashions and samples of the newest cloth. She always kept these on hand because the wealthy tourists who came in May knew of her fine work and kept her busy with their requests for the finest and fanciest dresses and gowns. Molly loved her work and it always seemed more a hobby than work to her.

Until now Catharine had not needed fine and fancy clothes here on the island. Unlike her mother, Elizabeth, Catharine preferred very light clothing so that the soft sea breezes could circulate and keep her skin cool, and they were loose-fitting with no tight waistbands or such to restrict the freedom of movement that she so loved. But that was about to change because she would be expected to be groomed grandly in London as befitted her grandfather's granddaughter and soon to be heir. It was hard for Catharine to sit for fittings and the like knowing that her Grandfather was so ill. And furthermore, since she had moved to the Outer Banks these types of clothes and things seemed so unimportant to her. But as she waited and made choices she knew that these were parts of her life that she must tend to with a spirit of love and respect, whether she liked it or not!

Elizabeth, Catharine's mother, had always been Molly's model customer. She dressed fashionably at all times, but she was smart enough to know that what worked in London fashion probably would have to be adjusted in order to become popular in the Outer Banks. So, she and Molly adjusted heavy fabrics to lighter ones. They lifted hemlines ever so slightly to allow more movement of the cooler air. They adjusted this and that until before they even realized, she and Molly had created their own brand of fashion. One that suited the Outer Banks clientele and one that was a hit with locals and tourists alike.

Tourists would always ask Molly if she could design a dress for them like Mrs. Chase wore to last week's fish-fry or did Molly have any more of the lovely fabric that she used for Mrs. Chase's beach-party dress. Yes, Elizabeth Chase was definitely a walking advertisement for Molly. But now Molly was going to outfit Elizabeth's daughter, who until now had only been interested in the simple fashions of comfort to be worn on the beaches of the "Banks" of North Carolina. However, Molly already knew in her mind many of the styles, fabrics and colors she would suggest that would be perfect for Catharine's new wardrobe.

Molly had the time of her life! She had always wanted to dress Catharine in some of the fancy new styles and dress materials and now, she would do just that. Her sewing machine, scissors, needles and ribbons flew. She had other ladies help her with hemming, sewing on buttons and snaps where she indicated, but the fine work and final touches she saw to herself and when her wardrobe was finished, Catharine was a beautiful sight to behold.

The new wardrobe was packed carefully in the trunk until the day they would be loaded on the ship which would carry them to London. There were softly scented sachets packed into folds of the gowns and undergarments, nightwear and slippers. Catharine and her mother went through their jewelry that they had brought to the islands, many had never been unwrapped, let alone worn. They matched each item to the gowns, some earrings, some necklaces, some brooches....

There was one thing that bothered Thomas and Elizabeth, Catharine's mother and father, and that was they needed a chaperone to accompany her on her trip. Thomas would make sure that she was always in the care of the ship's captain, but she still would need someone to accompany her. It would have been entirely unacceptable for a young, unmarried lady to travel alone on a long journey such as this. And that is when they all agreed they would ask Molly if she would accompany Catharine on this journey. Molly and Catharine had always been close friends and they would enjoy each other's company during the long boat ride. Molly was twenty five, a bit older than Catharine, and they felt she would be a perfect companion for her.

This at once made Catharine feel more comfortable. She had only imagined being on that ship, alone and homesick, for she knew she would be homesick! She had never been away from her Mother and Father, never away from her home or totally on her own before. But possibly Molly could be in the same boat! Molly and Catharine enjoyed being together and when they were alone they talked of things that all young girls talk of; love, marriage, children, just plain old girl talk. If Molly accompanied her, she and Molly would be there to encourage each other when those spells of homesickness came on them, and they would be there to laugh with each other at times too.

The next morning they all went to Molly's house with the hopes that she would agree to this long, but important trip. It was a hard subject to bring up because they all knew Molly and her parents would feel just the same way they felt about Catharine leaving home for a long time, in fact, none of them knew just how much time! When Molly's mother came to the door and greeted them she knew there was something unusual in the air, and that there was a mission involved here, but she had not a clue as to what that something was. After they talked about casual things for a few minutes they decided it was time to finally ask the question and get down to the business at hand. They knew it was a lot to ask for a young woman to up and leave her home for who knew how long, but they knew Molly was the person they needed right now. They were very anxious when they finally told her the reason for their visit. Finally, they said, here goes!

Molly was absolutely stunned. She had seldom been off the island, and had never set foot on a large ship. Her mother and father had come to the Outer Banks from Ireland when they were young and still had traces of an Irish accent, of which they were proud. They both were great storytellers and had told her volumes of Irish tales, many of which contained stories involving her family and her Irish roots. Like Catharine, Molly had never once thought of setting foot off this island. Her head was spinning. What in the world was she to do. But then she thought, "This is something I have only dreamed about."

She started to picture herself seeing the places of which she had only read, and she started believing that she was being presented with a gift that would only happen once in a lifetime. She looked at Catharine, who was like a sister to her, and they both started laughing! They stood up and hugged each other and danced around the floor in a circle like two children. They knew then that Molly would be with Catharine and they would each be there for the other to face whatever lay ahead.

Molly's mother and father were happy for her, but at the same time, they knew their daughter would be gone from them for who knows how long too, so it was a mixed bag. They were happy for her, but at the same time sad. However, they loved Catharine and her parents also, and they felt that Molly should be allowed to experience this once in a lifetime journey with a happy heart. They had made their decision. Molly would go with Catharine with their blessing!

Then a new situation arose. Molly would need a suitable wardrobe also. More head spinning... Molly's mother laughed, "We will just have a huge sewing bee. We will ask all the girls to help you and we will have a wardrobe made for you in no time."

And so it happened. There was not an idle moment for anyone involved until that ship left for England, with two lovely, finely dressed, young ladies aboard. One of them beautiful with dark hair and blue eyes, and one lovely with red hair with green eyes. Each so happy that they had the other to keep them from being too lonely and homesick. The ship's captain would be very attentive to their needs, as well as the entire crew, for they had been well paid to take care of these two very special travelers.

There was only one person whose heart was very heavy during all of the frantic preparations. Seth knew in his heart that it would be a long time before he would see Catharine again. The timing was so wrong, but there was nothing that he could do about it, nor would he have tried to stop it if he could, because he knew she was doing what she needed to do. It would not have been like Catharine to deny her grandfather what might be his final request of her.

Seth thought about the times they had talked and laughed together. How they seemed to be so at ease while talking together. Also, it seemed they liked so many of the same things. Except one thing, Catharine did not like Oysters and Seth loved them! How in the world could a beautiful girl like Catharine live on the Outer Banks and not like Oysters? He was just going to have to train her taste buds! He laughed out loud. I guess you can't have everything! But Oysters?

So many happy memories. He knew Catharine had to follow her heart and be with her Grandfather, but it all came about just when he discovered that he was in love....

CHAPTER SIX

(The Journey)

Catharine stood on the ship's deck thinking about leaving her mother and father behind, and this made her homesick already. They had never been apart before, making it overwhelming to know that she was responsible for herself for the first time in her life. And then, her thoughts turned to Seth. She had hated to tell him goodbye and she knew he felt the same way. There was something special going on there, but she wasn't ready to put a name to it yet. However, when they parted he had kissed her on the cheek and told her she would constantly be in his thoughts until she returned. Feelings she had not experienced were surfacing to be sure, but just what did it all mean....

She and Molly stood with arms linked as America faded from their view. There were surely mixed feelings right now. Some of those feelings were "I want to go back home right now." and some feelings were "Hurry to London! My Grandfather needs me right now." Probably the fact that life was going to get more complicated for them dawned on each of them right about now. They stood silently straining to catch the last glimpse of shoreline. But do you know that suddenly they were both filled with a happy anticipation of what lay ahead. A feeling that there would be exciting new first-time experiences for them both. And with that, they were shown to their rooms. Their hearts were lighter and they were optimistic. Also, they both were very tired. They'd had a long day filled with a roller coaster of emotions and they welcomed the sleep and rest which was right around the corner.

Meanwhile, Grandfather Chase had received the anxiously awaited response that his granddaughter and her chaperone and friend were en-route even then. He felt an instant pang of joy and of well-being just knowing she was on her way to visit. He immediately had his housekeepers and their helpers apply very special attention to the cleaning and shining of the large household. He had assigned the makeover of a special apartment, which had always been Catharine's, to be completely updated and ordered that nothing be spared to make it perfect. Then another apartment was to be done in like manner for her special friend and companion, Molly. Mr. Chase's house staff was so excited to have the young ladies visit and to have youth with all its energy in the house that it seemed like a royal holiday instead of added chores.

Chandeliers glistened and shone, banisters on the staircases almost sparkled, the beautiful hardwood floors wore such a shine that they looked dangerous to step on for fear of sliding across the large rooms. Rugs were beaten, pictures and portraits dusted, furniture waxed, and on top of all of this, food was constantly being prepared in the kitchen. Favorite recipes were being sorted through. They were asking each other to try to remember Catharine's favorite cake, pie, or any other type of food. Even Grandfather Chase got into the game. "Don't forget to make her favorite cake - the one her Grandmother Chase used to make." Grandfather Chase was the happiest he had been for many and many a day and everyone was busy making sure they left no stone unturned in preparation for the huge upcoming event.

Catharine and Molly had a fairly uneventful crossing to London. There were several storms that made them very thankful when they finally wore themselves out. Molly was especially glad because she found, to her dismay, that she was not a particularly good sailor. When the storms raged, she was completely out of order! Thankfully though, when the storms died, she pretty much returned to her old self. However, both ladies admitted that they would be glad when their feet were settled once again on dry land! Several children were sick with unnamed maladies for several days, but there were no serious setbacks and finally the "land ahoy" was heard. Everyone was so excited and busy finishing last minute packing and grooming that before they knew it, they were being taken ashore and her grandfather's welcoming party was waiting there to greet them.

Grandfather Chase had decided not to make the trip, but he was anxiously awaiting Catharine and Molly's arrival. The driver was there, and William, who was Grandfather's butler, as was his head housekeeper. All were there to meet them, and Catharine remembered them all so well, and her Grandfather's legal advisor, attorney and friend, Jake Parks, was also there. He said he was so pleased when Mr. Chase asked him to welcome Catharine and Molly in his stead and see that they were escorted back to him safely.

It was obvious that Jake Parks was well acquainted with Mr. Chase as he knew all about the stories of their lives since moving to the Outer Banks in America. He asked many questions and was so interested to hear both of their accounts regarding their lives in America that in no time it seemed they were driving down the handsome circular drive that lead to Grandfather Chase's grand home.

Molly was breathless. "Catharine, you never told me you once lived in such grandeur! I have only seen pictures of such. I didn't know that there really existed such perfection as this!" Molly couldn't comprehend how lawns were so manicured, not a blade of grass was ungroomed. The hedges were perfectly shaped and even the trees seemed to know they had to be just right to belong here. On the Outer Banks the grass and sea oats were pretty much left to their own devices. They helped to slow erosion from nor'easters, hurricanes, storms and such. They were wildly beautiful, but not manicured and tended as were these lawns.

When they entered the home, Molly just stared. She had never witnessed anything close to the beauty she saw here. Works of art hung from the walls, even the ceilings were masterpieces, and the furnishings from the windows to the floors were breathtaking. Catharine told her about several items that she knew would be of interest to her and gave her some time to just enjoy looking. Catharine was also enjoying the feeling of welcome she was experiencing. After all, she found she had missed the trappings of her old homeland too. The memories were rushing in and they were bringing to her feelings of contentment and nostalgia.

They then were carried up to their rooms to freshen up before meeting with Grandfather Chase. They came to Catharine's room first, and another gasp from Molly. Surely no person slept in such luxury. No one person enjoyed this much space and beauty. She opened the beautiful wardrobe and found it was filled with gowns and shoes, which Molly knew were the latest in fashion. The bureau drawers were filled with luxurious undergarments and all sorts of accessories such as hats, gloves and parasols, and on the bureau was a large and engraved wooden case filled with jewels. Molly just knew this was all a dream. She asked Catharine, "Whose clothes, shoes and jewels are these?" Catharine smiled and said, "I am just guessing, but I expect my grandfather had them all made in the hope that I would take him up on his offer to visit." Again, Molly can only shake her head in disbelief.

Then they went to the next room on the hall, which was Molly's room. It too had been totally refurbished in the most beautiful shades of green that Molly had ever seen. How had he known it was her favorite color? And, do you know what, her closet was also filled with clothes and her bureau with all the accessories too. Now how could he have known her shoe, dress and undergarment sizes! She would just have to find out about that. There was a dressing room adjacent to her room also, just like in Catharine's room.

She knew that she would only have a few minutes to take everything in before they would be called down to see Mr. Chase. Molly was really anxious to meet Grandfather Chase, but, she thought to herself, this has been a long day and I have never experienced so much excitement in one day in my whole life. "I am exhausted! I don't know if my feet will carry me another step!" But here comes Catharine with "let's go down and see Grandfather!" And I say to my feet, "Stay with me and let's go!"

CHAPTER SEVEN

(The Arrival)

Catharine was shocked when she first saw her grandfather sitting in his chair. He was looking out onto his beautiful garden, sitting very still, but he had a happy look on his face. She stood for just a minute to slowly take in the change that had occurred since she had seen him. Only a few years, but his health had been in a decline which had surely taken its toll. "Grandfather," Catharine said. He turned slowly and his face took on a new light that wasn't there before. He just looked at her for a time, studying her from head to toe and held both arms out, which Catharine rushed into as tears dripped from both their eyes. And from behind them, tears were gushing from Molly's eyes too. This was a scene to behold and she knew it. Her heart was bursting with happiness for both of them.

"Catharine, when you left here you were lovely, but while you have been away, you have grown beautiful. I have missed you so terribly each minute you have been away. I cannot wait to hear news of Thomas and Elizabeth. I hope they are well and that America has been all they hoped it would be! Thomas always liked exploring new and innovative ideas. He seemed to thrive when he was met with a challenge and I want to hear all about how he and Elizabeth have met all the challenges they must have had!"

"And speaking of beauty, and a redhead beauty at that, this must be Molly. Molly, welcome to my home. I am so happy that you were able to make the voyage with Catharine. I am looking forward to sitting down and talking with you about your Irish ancestors and your life in America. I hear, unlike Catharine, you were born in America and I want to hear about it all. Please make yourself at home while you are visiting, and if there is anything you need, you have only to ask. While you are here, I want you to consider yourself family! I will be introducing you to one of my favorite Irishmen shortly. He is a dear friend of mine and he also happens to be my doctor. His name is Patrick Kelly. Such a dedicated young doctor and a truer friend I haven't found. I hear your dad is a great Irish storyteller. So is Doctor Patrick. I am sure he will remember some of his Irish folklore tales while you are here and, unless I am wrong, I suspect you could tell him a few of your own that were handed down to you from your father."

"Ladies, come sit with me and tell me about your voyage. Was it smooth sailing? Were your quarters acceptable? Was the service and food as it should have been?" And so they were excited as they told him of their adventures aboard ship. Both girls shared their experiences, some of them hilarious and they found Grandfather Chase was thoroughly enjoying the visit. However, after an hour or so, they could tell he was tiring. So they told him that they were in need of a rest before dinner and asked him if he would excuse them. He apologized for not thinking of this and told them he would be looking forward to their dinner together so they could continue with their visit. "Dinner is at seven, and I have planned a very special one for you two. I will look forward to seeing you both at seven!"

While walking back to their rooms, Molly let it be known that she had fallen in love in the last hour! What a dear man Grandfather Chase was and how loving and kind. She just couldn't wait until dinnertime when they could all continue their visit. But, as they made their way to their rooms, they both realized that they were exhausted and that Grandfather Chase wasn't the only one in need of a rest. They said goodbye as they neared their rooms and each went in, spent a few minutes longing for home even in the midst of all this luxury, but then they both smiled happily and were asleep at once!

Dinner was lovely, the likes of which Molly had never before experienced. Cooks, maids, butlers, servers, were all storybook characters to her, but here they were in abundance. Every course was served exquisitely. Beautiful china and silver glittered and shone in the candlelight. Flowers were in abundance, beauty was everywhere and dinner was a delightful experience. The conversation never slowed because they were all so interested in each other's lives and had a lot of catching up to do.

After dinner they went into a smaller sitting room where

coffee was served. As they were getting seated Grandfather Chase's butler, William, entered the room and announced that they had a visitor. Jake Parks had stopped by to check on Mr. Chase and to see if he could be of any service to him or his guests. Grandfather Chase seemed pleased that he had come by and told William to send him right in. Catharine was slightly disappointed at the interruption, however. She had looked so forward to a relaxed evening and having a leisurely time for her and her grandfather to bring each other up to date with their lives. But Catharine could tell that her grandfather was pleased to have him come by and that he wanted she and Molly to have the chance to know him better.

Jake was a very striking young man who exuded perfect manners, and an air of well-being and confidence. He was dressed according to the latest fashion of the day and was considered to be one of London's most eligible and handsome bachelors. You could tell that Grandfather Chase and Jake were very comfortable with each other and that they knew each other very well. Jake knew all about Catharine's mother and father and he knew as much as Grandfather Chase did about their lives in America. He seemed so interested in her life there that Catharine soon found herself completely wrapped up in telling about her life on the Outer Banks of North Carolina.

He then questioned Molly about her life and seemed equally interested in her family, about her dressmaking talents, and about her long-standing friendship with Catharine. Soon Grandfather Chase was losing steam and noticeably wearing down, even though he was thoroughly enjoying the evening. He apologized to them and rang for William, saying he was sorry, but it was well past his bedtime. However, he told Jake and the girls to visit as long as they liked, but Jake, ever the polite gentleman, said he knew the girls were also weary from a long day and he also excused himself for the night, but assured them all that he would call soon and arrange a sightseeing excursion for them, and asked if that met with their approval. They both agreed that it was a great gesture and especially for Molly who had never seen London. Jake said she must have a first-rate tour of London and he would be in touch soon. With that, he said goodnight to the ladies and was gone.

Molly, who had never before seen such elegance before in a man, was smitten. Catharine, who HAD seen such elegance before, was NOT smitten. She had suspected an overstated attention to her grandfather and she herself noticed something, a glance, a slightly too long eye contact, just something. Of course, she didn't share this with Molly. Molly who was a smart girl, would find all these things out for herself in time. But not tonight! As soon as Jake was seen to the door, they both decided to follow Grandfather Chase's example and retire. However, Catharine was searching to find out what was causing this strange feeling. It wasn't like her to be judgmental without reason and Jake had really not given her a valid reason to doubt his character like this. But Catharine was not comfortable at all....

And this strange feeling had made her homesick for the first time since she arrived in London. She thought of her mother and father. She wondered if Seth's sister and brother-in-law,

Sarah and Abe, had had their baby yet? Was it a boy or a girl? If it had been born, what was his or her name? She thought about all of her neighbors and friends on the Outer Banks and how they were so appreciative of simple things. How their main cares were centered around each other, their well-being, and their families. And she thought about Seth. She missed him. "Oh My! I am getting homesick!", she thought to herself.

But try as she may, her memories returned to thoughts of Seth. Memories that got sweeter as time passed. Mentally she compared Seth to the dandified men she was in contact with now. Seth was a man who was completely trustworthy. His concerns were not focused on his own personal appearance or his own personal comforts but on the needs of his family and his community. He was more focused on the lives, needs and comforts of others. She tried to compare the person who was Seth to the person who was Jake but she couldn't. There just was no comparison to be made between the two men or any of the men she had known when she lived in London.

One of Molly's greatest surprises was that she, because she was Catharine's guest and best friend, was treated with the same regard as Catharine. Her room was straightened and her bed made daily for her. Her clothes perfectly laundered and ironed, the maids were constantly checking to see if there was anything more she needed. Her bath was set up for her every day, and so on it went. This was a lot to get used to if you had never before been pampered like this. But, she thought, I believe I could get used to it!

Catharine and Molly were on their way down to have breakfast with Grandfather Chase several days later. They always had breakfast with him in his room because it was easier for him in the mornings than coming to the dining room. He was served his meal on a tray on his bed, and Catharine and Molly ate from trays set up on either side of the bed. This worked wonderfully because with one sitting on one side of him and one on the other, they were all close enough to talk with ease. During these breakfasts they learned many things about each other and, in fact, it was one of the most enjoyable times of the day for them, because Grandfather Chase usually was more alert and energetic in the mornings. Just as they were finishing breakfast, William came in to say they had a visitor. Mr. Jake Parks....

CHAPTER EIGHT

(The Outing)

Jake had come to say that since it was such a beautiful sunshiny day, he wondered if the ladies would like to make a day of it by visiting the various attractions of the city. He also said that since London is not particularly known for its abundance of sunshiny days, one needed to take advantage of them. Grandfather Chase said he hoped the ladies would be in agreement because they would enjoy the fresh air and sunshine and would also enjoy each other's company. He said, "I know these ladies get tired of the same old boring company that they get daily doses of here!" One couldn't help but get the message that Grandfather Chase was maybe doing a little matchmaking here? Anyway, Jake asked if ten o'clock would be enough time for them to get ready for the day and they both agreed it would. He said that, until then, he had several items he needed to discuss with Mr. Chase.

Grandfather Chase then asked if after their day of sightseeing Jake would stay and have dinner with them and Jake said he would very much enjoy that. With that, the ladies retired to get ready for their sightseeing trip and Jake and Grandfather Chase prepared for their discussion of business. They would have to hurry. What fun! What young lady doesn't enjoy donning beautiful new frocks!

Both Catharine and Molly enjoyed choosing from their newly acquired fancy dresses. They both opted to wear one of the lovely gowns provided by Grandfather Chase. They both knew these gowns were at the height of fashion, since he had chosen only the most sought-after dressmakers in London. They agreed it would please him when they appeared for their outing wearing them, and also he could take pride as they went out and about in London representing his family so beautifully! They would definitely make him proud.

Catharine had chosen a white dress embroidered with small sprigs of lavender flowers and with a matching lavender satin sash perfectly matching both the flowers in her dress and the color of her eyes. Molly chose, of course, a soft green gown with slightly darker green satin sash, which was perfect with her red hair and made her green eyes sparkle even more.

Finally, they were ready to meet Jake for their day of excitement. They met Jake in Grandfather's room and both gentlemen gave them a rousing once-over saying they were "breathtaking!" Grandfather telling Jake to be sure everyone they met knew they were of his family and Jake told him not to worry about that because he had never been in the company of not even one beauty such as these, but two, well that was just too grand! They hugged Grandfather goodbye and told him they would see him at dinner. What good medicine these girls were for him. Jake told them he had never seen him this happy. And so, the three of them were off to see the sights.

Molly was so excited to see all of the things she had only read about. Her eyes sparkled and there was nothing that they saw that didn't interest her. Jake said she was the perfect person to introduce to the sights of London. Most people were interested in only the highlights of the city, but Molly seemed to want to learn it all. Not only that, but she wanted to learn it all in one day! Her enthusiasm was catching and soon Catharine and Jake found they were seeing the city as if they too had never seen it. They found they were searching for small details that they had never before thought about. What a fun day they had, and Jake was a wonderful host.

At noon they stopped for lunch at a lovely café and Jake made selections from the menu of an assortment of specialties that he felt the ladies would enjoy. He handled these sorts of decisions for them with such an ease, that they both appreciated just enjoying the meal without having the responsibility to choose. They talked of things involving London and its history, and Jake seemed to be so knowledgeable about these things that both ladies enjoyed the stories he so eloquently related.

But all too soon it was time to move on to the next phase

of their adventure. And then, long before they were ready for the day to end, Jake announced that they would need to leave the rest for another day in order to return home in time for dinner with Grandfather Chase. On the trip home they relived the day and Molly was so appreciative to both Catharine and Jake for being such knowledgeable guides. She had never once expected she would see or visit these world-famous sites and Catharine and Jake, who knew this city so well, made this experience even more perfect.

But as they drove around the beautiful circular drive toward the mansion there was a great commotion which was evident to everyone there. Catharine knew immediately that something was wrong, as they all did. Jake brought the carriage to a halt and they all began running toward the house to see what was the matter. As they came to the front door William met them and said that Mr. Chase had had an awful spell of some sort. He had gone in to check on him and found him unable to respond and had called his doctor. His doctor, Patrick Kelly, a young Irishman who Grandfather Chase had become very fond of, had come at once and decided that Mr. Chase needed to be transported to the hospital.

The ambulance had been called and they were in the process of transporting the patient. Jake, who knew Doctor Kelly, asked him what was happening, and Doctor Kelly told him that it appeared that Mr. Chase may have had a stroke. He wouldn't elaborate on how serious he felt his condition was at that time, and suggested that they could follow them to the hospital where further tests would help them to determine the extent of the damage done.

Time seemed to stand still until they arrived at the hospital and Grandfather Chase was taken into the emergency section. Nurses and doctors were buzzing around with everyone having their specific roles to play. But it soon dawned on them that the only course for them was to patiently wait, for it could be a long time before they had any answers.

THE BLACK PELICAN

PART III

CHAPTER NINE

(Greed - A Sad Story)

The evening dragged and just when Jake, Catharine and Molly decided they were hungry and needed a snack, Doctor Kelly came out to give them a much anticipated update. He spoke to Catharine and in a very serious voice told her that her Grandfather had suffered a severe attack and because he was so weak he was very fortunate to have come through it. Doctor Kelly would not elaborate on what caused this attack but said they were running every available test to get to the bottom of the cause of this newest problem.

Doctor Kelly also said that he would require complete bed rest until they were able to determine how best he would respond to medications and treatments. He suggested she hire a nurse to tend to him around the clock upon his release from the hospital. He continued, you may feel that you want to be the one to tend to him, but you cannot give him the professional attention he is going to need. I will be keeping a close watch over him here in the hospital until I feel he is ready to make the move home, but I cannot tell you right now how long that might be. Catharine, you know that Mr. Chase is much more than a patient to me, he is a dear friend. You can rest assured that I will see that he is given the best treatment available. Then he held the sobbing Catharine who after a moment or so gained her composure and felt comforted and more hopeful.

Catharine then told Patrick Kelly how much it meant to her to know he was there for her Grandfather and how she knew he would be so much more at ease just knowing his friend, Doctor Kelly, was near. She told him that she would begin searching for nursing care for him the very next day, and she thanked him again for being there in their time of need. It seemed her life was taking fast and furious turns and each decision seemed more drastic and complicated than the one before. Where in the world did you turn to find qualified nurses? How would she know whether or not they were, in fact, qualified? She silently asked for wisdom and strength....

Doctor Kelly suggested that they all go home to eat and that they get some rest, and if there was a change during the night they could be assured he would contact them. Catharine asked if she could see her Grandfather for a minute and Patrick agreed to let her go in for just one moment. When she saw her Grandfather her heart was aching. As far as she knew, he was not aware that she was even there, but she spoke lovingly to him and kissed his much loved face and told him that she would always be there for him, no matter what! This latest event made her so thankful that she and Molly had made the trip to London. She was so thankful that she was able to be by his side when he needed her most and she must also remember to tell Molly over and over again what a blessing she had been to her on this trip.

This Catharine did on the drive home from the hospital. In no uncertain terms she told Molly that she didn't know if she could have faced all of these huge challenges without her. Molly who had always loved Catharine and had come to love Grandfather Chase as her own grandfather simply said to Catharine that she was now a part of their family. She would never be just a best friend anymore, but from now on they were much more. They were now the sisters that neither of them ever had! They both wept.

When they arrived home, the entire household was still up hoping to hear some news from the hospital. They had prepared a supper for them, not knowing whether or not they had eaten, they all ate ravenously because neither of the three had eaten since lunchtime. Catharine was touched by the dedication and love they showed her grandfather. She told them all she knew. She told them about Doctor Kelly's orders for around-the-clock nursing care, which she would start to seek out in the morning. She thanked them all for their love and concern and also for their unwavering loving care for her Grandfather. Then she told them to get a good night's sleep because starting in the morning they all would have adjustments to make and she would need all of their help.

Jake had been close at hand every day and night since Catharine and Molly had arrived. He had not tried to hide the fact that he had feelings for Catharine, but he was too smart not to know that this was not the time to pursue those feelings. Daily he came and went, taking care of Grandfather's business interests and each day visiting Grandfather, if only for a short while. Catharine thought to herself, when Grandfather is feeling better, I will start getting into and learning about these business interests. I need to learn all areas of his holdings, since Grandfather says they have already been signed over to me.

Jake, after asking if there was anything more he could do for them, left for the night. Catharine and Molly were exhausted from the long day which started out with their grand sightseeing excursion, but which surely had not ended up like they would have hoped. They headed to their apartments for much-needed rest and to let their minds roam over the many events of the day. But they were tired, and soon they both slept.

They both woke up to the delicious aromas of breakfast being prepared. Both girls decided right away that they were hungry and it didn't take them long to prepare themselves for it! Everyone seemed to be working as if they had a special purpose for this day. And it seemed that the special purpose was to help in any way they could to make the changes they had talked about come about as easily as possible. Just as they were starting breakfast, William came in to announce a visitor, Doctor Patrick Kelly. Patrick had come by on his way to the hospital to tell them that Mr. Chase had had a quiet night, which was good since the first forty-eight hours after a serious attack such as this was such a critical time. He seemed in such high spirits over this news that when asked if he would join them for breakfast he said, "I believe I will!"

Catharine couldn't help but notice that Molly seemed very hesitant and shy at the table this morning. She also couldn't help but notice that the Doctor had a little more red in his face than usual too. Had she been missing something? One could not fail to notice that the good doctor and Molly definitely had eyes for each other.... This was a fun turn of events and would bear close watching!

Then, as if finally remembering his mission in the first place, Patrick got to the main reason for his visit. "Catharine," he said, "I know you said you were going to start your search for nurses for Mr. Chase this morning. I don't know if you have any prospects as of yet, but I happen to know and would like to suggest a very efficient nurse who is currently on leave from the hospital. Her name is Mrs. King. She has recently lost her husband but is now ready to return to nursing. I thought, if you are interested, I could suggest to her that you two meet and get to know each other. I feel that possibly this could be an arrangement that might work for each of you. She would, I'm sure, be more interested in working during the day, and if this works, I believe it would take care of the most critical portion of your search."

Catharine was almost in tears with gratitude for Patrick's suggestion. He said he would set up an agreeable time for them to meet and would be back in touch. He also told her that Mrs. King might know of a second nurse who could fill the night spot.

Usually people in the profession know of any reliable people who are available. This was all such good news to Catharine because she really was at a loss as to where to start to look for the best help available, and now Patrick Kelly was offering not only his help, but his professional opinion. Now she and Molly could dress and go to the hospital to check on her favorite Grandfather!

CHAPTER 10

(The New Nurse Arrives & A New Courtship Begins)

Just as Doctor Kelly promised, he arranged a meeting between Mrs. King and Catharine for the following day. Mrs. King was a middle aged lady who was at once perceived by Catharine as a perfect fit for the position of nursing her grandfather. She was energetic, very professional, of a happy nature and, most of all, as they talked about prior nursing duties, she showed a true feeling of compassion for her patients. So much so that Catharine knew Patrick Kelly had presented to her a choice that would work out just fine. Catharine and Mrs. King agreed that she would start her nursing position as soon as she was able. Catharine felt it would be best for them all if she could come in before Grandfather came home from the hospital and become familiar with the staff, with the daily schedule, with the house, and even with Grandfather's room. During that time she could decide if there were any additional items needed to make her Grandfather more comfortable or to make her work easier. She agreed to come the next day, since she was in total agreement with the wisdom of Catharine's plan.

Mrs. King also agreed to talk with a young nurse that she had occasion to work with before and who, in her opinion, was totally dependable and knowledgeable. Catharine was thankful for this additional help, being well aware that she had no experience at all in this area. Another problem seemingly solved!

Now Doctor Patrick Kelly was a typical Irishman. Red hair, green eyes, and a boisterous nature that endeared him to his patients and, for that matter, to all who came in contact with him. And, as he did when finding Mrs. King for Catharine, he helped his patients in ways that were sometimes beyond what you would expect of your doctor. He called at the house every day to give the latest updates on Grandfather Chase, which was completely unneeded, as Catharine and Molly were at the hospital daily! But, by now, Catharine knew he had two reasons for his daily visit. And Molly always managed to be near at hand when he arrived.

Finally the day came when he asked Molly to have dinner with him. There was a special affair that he wanted to attend on the next Friday, and he said he would be so pleased if she would attend with him. He blushed as red as fire when he asked her. Molly was so excited and speechless that Catharine thought she might have to accept for her. Finally, Molly found her tongue and said she would love to go with him. She asked all the right questions like how formal the affair was, so she would know what to wear, and so on, and so the romance began.

Well, that evening you could feel the happiness in that house. Everybody's spirits seemed to be lifted. Finally, something to feel happy about was happening in this house! Of course, Doctor Patrick Kelly had already won the hearts of the entire household. Even Mrs. King who had been developing a mutually respected working relationship with Doctor Patrick for a long time, and who had lost her husband during the past year, was happy to feel a boost to her spirits.

Something else was happening that lifted the spirits of everybody in that house. Doctor Kelly was releasing Grandfather Chase from the hospital. Mrs. King had suggested they install a hospital bed in Grandfather's room so his bed positions could be adjusted, and which would make him much more comfortable. This had been installed already, another of the things that made Catharine realize how much of a difference Mrs. King's efficient and professional planning had made during the past few days, and how much easier things go when you are well prepared.

Grandfather Chase was a weak man when he returned home, but seemingly gaining strength every day, and he was so happy to be there. Mrs. King saw to it that he wanted for nothing. She seemed to know just how to please him and how to help ease any distress he was experiencing. In no time, the gleam had come back into his eyes and he was gaining ground. Catharine felt so thankful and when she wrote her update to her mother and father, her joy and relief was obvious to them too. She wrote at length about Mrs. King's wisdom concerning her patient and how she seemed to know just the right things to say and do that were making Grandfather Chase's recovery so much easier. She also asked about Seth.....

That next week the whole household participated in the planning to make sure Molly had everything she needed for a perfect night with Doctor Patrick. And on Friday, they ironed the dress that she chose to wear (a beautiful green to match those eyes, of course), they prepared an extravagant bath for her, and helped her dress. And additionally, one of the girls who was particularly talented with creating popular hair styles of the day, piled that beautiful red hair in natural ringlets high on her head. Catharine brought in a set of earrings with a matching necklace for Molly that she just knew would be the perfect accessories for that green dress. Molly hugged Catharine and asked her how she knew that she hadn't been able to find just the right jewelry to wear with her dress. When finally she was ready, the finished product was lovely. She was ready for the biggest night of her life and she was so nervous, but first she had one last thing to do before Patrick arrived.

She went downstairs to see Grandfather Chase. Molly knew he was excited about her big night out with Doctor Patrick Kelly, and she did not disappoint. Grandfather had her turn this way and that so that he would not miss seeing any angle of this lovely young lady. He found that he had come to love her as an additional granddaughter. And there obviously was someone else who was totally smitten by Molly, and that was the good Doctor.

There was a small knock at the door and it was Catharine.

When she came into the room, she just beamed to see such a beautiful Molly and she told her, "Molly, Patrick will not be able to speak when he sees how beautiful you are tonight!" Molly laughed because she had never before been fussed over like this and she was feeling so special right now.

Molly kissed Grandfather goodnight and told him that in the morning she would share every detail with him. Then she went up to her apartment to get her wrap.

At just that time, William was at the door and Patrick had arrived. Patrick was so handsome as he stood at the doorway, even William almost whistled (but, of course, being the proper butler that he was, he did not. He only wished he could have!). Patrick asked William if he could see Grandfather Chase for a minute or two and William led the way to Grandfather Chase's room. Well, Grandfather Chase did **try** to whistle, but couldn't. He did tell Patrick that the other couples may as well stay home tonight because there was no question as to who the loveliest couple would be at this affair!

Doctor Patrick told Grandfather that he wanted him to know he would take good care of Molly tonight. He also told him that he cared a great deal for her and he hoped Grandfather didn't disapprove of her going out with him. Grandfather laughed at this. It felt like Patrick was asking his permission to take a daughter or granddaughter out and it made him feel proud that Patrick would do this. Patrick said goodnight to Grandfather who told him, "Now take a deep breath, son, for she is going to take your breath away."

And he was speechless and breathless. When Molly came down the stairway, Patrick was perfectly still and perfectly quiet. He didn't seem able to break his gaze from the beauty slowly coming toward him. Finally, he gained his tongue and simply said, "Molly, you are just beautiful." And let me tell you, Molly was just as smitten by Doctor Patrick. And she said to him, "Thank you Doctor Patrick, and you are very handsome tonight yourself." They both laughed at each other's clumsy compliment attempts. He placed her wrap around her shoulders and they were off.

It was the first time they had ever been alone together. At first they were quiet, with conversation not coming easy for either of them. But once they broke the silence, it seemed they had been close friends forever. They knew immediately that they had so many things in common and that their interests were shared so much so that they were at once at ease. The problem was that they arrived all too soon at their destination, long before they had hardly started their life stories. But these things would have to wait for a while....

Needless to say, Doctor Patrick and Molly were the toast of that London party. There was not a person there who wasn't enchanted by this handsome couple. And Molly was the belle of the ball with her beauty and impeccable dress. Also being a guest at the home of Mr. Thomas Chase didn't hurt a thing! But what, more than anything, that won hearts and garnered attention was the genuineness of this beautiful girl.

She was not pretentious. She loved telling stories of her

beloved Outer Banks of North Carolina. She told of the simple lifestyle of her people and of their simple goodness and how they cared for each other daily, but especially when they were in need. I'll tell you, she had converted many a person into thinking of taking a boat ride to see those "Outer Banks" for themselves!

And when the evening ended and she and Dr. Patrick thanked their hosts and left for home, all in attendance knew they had spent the evening with a couple of "quality"!

On the way home Molly and Doctor Patrick talked so easily of many things, but besides being totally mesmerized by Molly, Doctor Patrick was enchanted by tales of her beloved "Outer Banks." He wanted to know every detail about the place and about the people who lived there. Molly told him many things, but there wasn't time to tell him all of the stories, such as the potluck dinner by the beach, where it was so obvious Seth and Catharine were falling in love! Both this night and that night ended far too soon....

After Molly and Dr. Patrick reluctantly said their good-nights, Catharine was excitedly waiting to hear all about Molly's evening. They even had a cup of tea together while they went over all of the little details.

Most of the people Molly met at the party knew Catharine before her family had moved to the Outer Banks, and newcomers knew of her as they learned of her family's longstanding history in London. Everybody had sent their best wishes for her and for her Grandfather. Molly told each of them that Catharine had not taken the time for a social life since she had arrived in London, since she had spent almost all of her waking hours by her Grandfather's side, and attending to his every need. But, Molly told them that Grandfather Chase was improving wonderfully and this alone was enough to boost Catharine and the entire household's spirits.

Now it was time for Catharine's good news. She just couldn't hold back any longer from telling Molly this happy news. Mrs. King, the wonderful nurse recommended to her by Doctor Patrick seemed to be working somewhat of a miracle with Grandfather Chase. He seemed to be gaining strength daily and was even walking a little bit, with Mrs. King's and Catharine's assistance. Even Doctor Patrick agreed that this was amazing! "So now, Molly, you can go back to telling me about your evening with Doctor Patrick, but I couldn't wait another minute to tell you about Grandfather's good news for the day!"

Molly told Catharine how attentive Doctor Patrick had been to her all night. Even though she had not known a soul at this beautiful event, she never felt like she didn't belong because he was always right by her side. To which Catharine told her, "Molly, you don't realize how much people are drawn to you! You are so easy to talk with that Doctor Patrick could have left the room and you still would have been at ease. You still would have been okay. You will make a wonderful doctor's wife!" At this last remark, Molly's face flushed so that it was pretty near to the color of her beautiful head of hair! "Catharine," she said, "We have just been out one time! I do like Doctor Patrick far more than anyone I have ever met, but to talk of being his wife? My goodness! It is time for us to go to bed. We have both gotten addle-brained!" And with this they both had a good, much needed laugh.

Catharine then told Molly that she had more good news, which she had saved until she had heard the entire story about Molly's evening. Catharine had received letters from home today. Her eyes lit with excitement. One of the letters was from Seth! He had written to tell her that Sarah and Abe had a new baby daughter. He was an uncle! They had named her Anna, and her middle name was Catharine! Seth said they had used Catharine as her middle name because they hoped she would grow up to have the character that they loved in Catharine. He had asked Catharine's mother and father not to write her about this, but to wait and let him write and tell her the good news.

She could feel the joy and pride in his letter. He told her that he missed her and that he hoped she missed him too. He told her to hurry home as soon as she was able. He told her nothing was the same without her. It made her so homesick that she felt she couldn't stand to be away from the Outer Banks another minute... yet she knew she must. She would fulfill her promise to herself and to her Grandfather!

But maybe someday soon she would be able to take that long-awaited trip home! To the land, to the ones, and to the one, that she loved.... Did she just think that? Did she allow herself to think that? "I guess I am really tired!"

Catharine had also received a letter from her Mother and

Father with news about this and that, but she couldn't keep her mind on anything but Seth's letter and what he had told her about missing her, about nothing being the same without her... Molly told her, "Catharine, you talk about me being a "wife", it sounds to me like it is me hearing these sounds of love from you, or is that just something I *thought* I saw on the night of the potluck dinner. Did I just dream that, or what?" Catharine says, "I think we are both exhausted! We have started talking foolish! We need to get some rest!" And with another good laugh, they headed to bed, but they both surely had a lot on their minds. A lot to think about....

CHAPTER 11

(The Day of Discovery)

The next morning, Catharine knew the time had come when she needed to be knowledgeable about and a part of the decision-making in her Grandfather's business ventures, and she needed to know these things inside and out.

Jake arrived soon after they had finished breakfast and said he would be busy for most of the day catching up on some areas of business that he felt he hadn't found time to keep on top of, with all of the excitement and changes that had taken place lately. He visited with Grandfather for a few minutes and was taking his leave to go into Grandfather's office when Catharine said to him that she would like to start working with him today so she could begin to come up-to-date on the status of Grandfather's business affairs.

Jake was noticeably taken by surprise with this announcement. He had had full rein of these books and all business affairs for a long time now and it didn't go unnoticed that this was not a path he would have chosen. However, Grandfather spoke up and said he thought that would be a splendid idea, since all decisions were ultimately in Catharine's very capable hands now. This left Jake no alternative but to agree to this new, however unwelcome, arrangement.

Catharine noticed that while this visit was taking place, Mrs. King never left her chair which was sitting right beside Grandfather's bed. In fact, she never left the room when anyone came or went when visiting Grandfather Chase. This was very noticeable Catharine thought, because she remembered usually nurses would leave the room when a visitor arrived.

Molly was on her way down for her morning visit with Grandfather when she met Catharine who told her she would be in Grandfather's office with Jake for at least the rest of the morning. She asked Molly if she would keep an open ear for any assistance Mrs. King might need today, and said that she had told Mrs. King to contact Molly if she needed anything while Catharine was in Grandfather's office with Jake. She told her that she needed to learn all she could about Grandfather's business affairs and from now on, she would ask to be kept up-do-date on everything. Molly knew this would mean that their time together would be more limited now and it made her sad, but she knew it had to be done because Catharine was not a person to do anything half way. Besides, she was more than happy to spend more time with Grandfather Chase and Mrs. King.

Catharine had hoped for an orderly and complete introduction to the different aspects of Grandfather's affairs. One look and she could see this probably was not going to happen. Catharine noticed that Jake was uncomfortable for some reason when asked questions regarding specific areas. She thought he probably was uncomfortable having to explain business to a female. Didn't everybody know women should not, and did not, know anything about business? Didn't they know women couldn't handle it? This was Catharine's excuse, in her own mind, for Jake's discomfort.

However, this was not entirely the case. It only took a little while for Jake to realize that Catharine was very astute in things of business. She even explained to him that before she moved to America, her Grandfather had taken great pride in teaching her to be a smart businesswoman, and she had sat with him for many hours pouring over his books. In fact, since her Grandfather's first love at that time was his business, this was when she had spent her favorite hours with him and, she always believed, she gained immeasurable respect in his eyes at that time. Yes sir! His Granddaughter, like her old Grandfather, had a keen eye for business! Catharine's father had felt this was a very wise decision also, so he too took advantage of her keen business mind.

By lunchtime, they had explored several areas of investments and many property deeds, each entailing vast fortunes, and they hadn't scratched the surface yet. Catharine knew even by that time she would be involved in a very complicated and time consuming lifestyle if she chose to handle this vast fortune personally. She then and there decided that managing a fortune day-in and day-out was not how she wanted to spend her life. She would learn the ropes and decide how best to handle it all at a future time. Right now, she would keep all of this to herself and keep her mind and eyes open in order to make the right decision.

When lunchtime came, Jake apologized to Catharine and told her he had a previous engagement for the afternoon, but he would return in the morning and they could take up where they left off. This suited Catharine to a tee. She felt she had taken in enough for one day. She thanked Jake for his help and followed him to the door.

After lunch, Catharine decided she wanted to go back into Grandfather's office and just randomly go over some entries and papers. She felt she needed to familiarize herself totally with the system that was in place. As she scanned through the different entries she found she was confused by some of the entries and also confused by the lack of some entries. She didn't worry overmuch. She just figured she didn't have the total picture yet and it would all come together as they progressed forward. Still, the picture that was developing always had the same outcome. Funds, deeds and official papers missing always meant a loss to the estate of Grandfather Chase. Go rest, Catharine. Your mind is tired. You need rest! But, be careful....

There were several things Catharine thought about today which were a puzzlement to her. One was the fact that Jake said this morning that he would be in the office the rest of the day in order to catch up on some things he had gotten behind on in the past few weeks. Then, when Catharine had said she would like to sit in with him as he worked, he suddenly remembered he had a previous engagement for the afternoon? Another puzzlement, why did Mrs. King never leave Grandfather Chase's bedside? And where were the pieces missing from Grandfather's files? And Grandfather suddenly seems to be miraculously gaining ground health wise! And another thing, while we are at it....

"Wait! I need to talk with Doctor Patrick!"

As it happened several nights a week, Doctor Patrick came by to check on Grandfather Chase, and it so happened, he thankfully came by on this night. After he checked Grandfather, they chatted for a short while and Doctor Patrick said his goodbyes to each one. Molly and Catharine rose to go with him to the door, which was unusual, because they all knew he wanted to spend a few precious minutes with Molly before he left. However, on this night Catharine followed them out of Grandfather's room. When they were outside of the room, Catharine asked Doctor Patrick if she could have a private word or two with him and, of course, he agreed. Molly left them alone to talk, probably thinking that Catharine had questions regarding the care of her Grandfather or the like.

She apologized to Doctor Patrick for taking his time, but she assured him that she was concerned about a few things that she hoped he could help her with. She thanked him for his continuing care for her Grandfather and she thanked him profusely for sending Mrs. King to them. She made every minute of the day so much easier for all of them. Then she told him that she had several questions which were very, very personal and that bothered her to speak of, but that she needed an answer to, if he could provide one.

She asked about the strange behavior of Mrs. King who absolutely never left the side of her Grandfather, even when he had visitors in the room. Doctor Patrick answered without hesitation that this was done strictly according to his instructions. Doctor Patrick told her that he had instructed Mrs. King to never allow Grandfather Chase to be alone with anyone! He also said to Catharine that he had good reason for this.

He had been wanting to speak with Catharine about this, but he said he had felt the timing was not right and that he had not had sufficient evidence until now to warrant these actions. However, he said that certain tests had come back to the hospital which revealed that there was a slight trace of a poisonous substance in her Grandfather's blood. Which, when Catharine heard, she gasped in horror! He told her that her Grandfather's life may be in serious jeopardy and that every precaution possible should be taken to make sure that he was kept safe from a possible predator. Someone who may have reason to take his life!

This was such a devastating revelation to Catharine that she was speechless. Never in her lifetime had she ever thought anyone would want to do her Grandfather harm. And especially when everyone thought he was nearing the end of his life and couldn't possibly have an enemy in the world. This, however, was evidently not the case. Doctor Patrick told Catharine that she and the trusted members of her household staff must be constantly alert and protective of her Grandfather.

It was at this point that Catharine shared with Doctor Patrick some of the other concerns that were on her mind. She shared with Patrick some of the events of the day she had just spent with Jake. She told him of the missing information in some areas of the files to which she had just been introduced. She told him that all of these inconsistencies were detrimental to her Grandfather's holdings and that Jake was very uncomfortable while they were working together examining the entries to these files. Also, that he said he had a prior engagement right at lunchtime when he had said earlier that he wanted to work all afternoon to catch up with his work on the files.

Then, finally, Catharine said that she had noticed the magical improvement in her Grandfather's health. She was so thankful for this, but it seemed miraculous and she asked Doctor Patrick if he had been giving him a new medication or if he had any indication as to why his condition was so improved? Doctor Patrick told her flatly that he believed Mr. Chase was improving so steadily because whoever was responsible for the traces of poison in his system no longer had free access to him, his food or his drink. This was allowing his body to rid itself of those substances that were slowly taking his life and his body was daily restoring itself to health.

Catharine's mind was moving in a direction she didn't like.

She was drawing a conclusion, not yet proven, but the thoughts she was having were making her sick! It couldn't be true, could it? No one would try to poison an old man who thought you were so special, would they? She would just have to think about all of this later. However, she was aware that she needed to be alert to the possible danger to them all.

Doctor Patrick told Catharine as truthfully as he knew how that he did not have all of the answers now. But, he also told her to keep her eyes open and let him know of any new developments as she saw them. He also told her to inform Molly of their talk and to ask her to keep a watchful eye. Catharine said she would do this and, after a long, weary day, she and Dr. Patrick said goodnight. Molly was still waiting her turn to say goodnight to the good Doctor too!

Dr. Patrick and Molly were sorry to have to part tonight. It was one of those times when you wanted to hold on to someone you loved for a long, long time. There were things going on in this usually serene household and no one was well enough informed of all the facts to feel they had a handle on the problem, let alone to know where to begin to fix it.

Catharine and Molly were both ready to retire because, as usual, their day had been long, hard and confusing. They agreed to meet in the morning for a talk after they had their usual visit with Grandfather Chase. They both knew they wanted and needed to talk about developing concerns, but tonight they were too spent to think clearly and any decision they arrived at now might not be the right one. They hugged each other tightly and told each other how thankful they were to have each other's friendship and love.

But, when Catharine got into bed, she found she came wide awake. Too many unbelievable things were dashing around in her head. Sleep would not come. Then she had an idea about how she might deal with some of her problems. She needed to discuss with someone everything that was going on here in London. She needed someone who would not have any agenda but to listen to what she had to say. She knew who that person was and she got out her pen and paper and started to write.

And at once she felt relief. She felt she had made a right decision and just like that she began to write:

CHAPTER 12

(Help!)

Dear Seth,

I do so miss you since I have been in London. There are so many decisions to be made and I am feeling inadequate when it comes to making all of them. There are so many good people who depend on the wisdom of my actions. I never knew that making day-to-day decisions could be so difficult. Can I bend your ear? You don't have to feel any responsibility with regard to giving me answers or help, I just feel I need to talk with someone that I utterly trust.

There are so many questions that need answers, so I will start with Grandfather's health. He is improving unbelievably fast, so much so that we are all amazed, including his fantastic doctor, Doctor Patrick Kelly. We have acquired a heaven-sent nurse, Mrs. King, who sits with Grandfather days and we have a younger nurse who was recommended by Mrs. King, who sits with him nights. Neither of them leaves his bedside, even when he has company. Never. This is because of instructions by Doctor Patrick. When Grandfather was in the hospital there were a series of tests done and one of them discovered a trace of a poisonous substance in his blood. Doctor Patrick says it was a very slight amount, but that over a period of time it could lead to severe problems, and even to death! Therefore, he instructed the nurses to, under no circumstances, leave his bedside with another person present.

This was immediately done. Now Mrs. King is a sweet lady for sure, but she is a dragon-lady where her patient is concerned, and then the strangest thing started to occur. Almost daily Grandfather's condition started to improve. He is even walking some now, with Mrs. King's help. This is a wonderful change, but it has Doctor Patrick wondering if someone may have been slipping a poisonous substance into his food or drink!

On another entirely different front, today I worked in Grandfather's office with Jake Parks. I know that I should be keeping up with the many other areas of his estate, which he says is now mine. I have always liked to be included in the business affairs of both my Grandfather and my Father. They have always interested me. However, I can assure you that the estate we are talking about is on a whole new level and branches out in so many directions that it makes my head spin!

We only worked during the morning because after Jake had said he wanted to work all day in an effort to start to catch up on some paperwork concerning the accounts, when we started going over the accounts, he suddenly decided that he had an appointment for the afternoon and he would have to cut our planned working time short. To tell you the truth, I was ready for a much needed break anyway.

Seth, did I mention to you that by this time my head was spinning!

I realize that I am no professional when it comes to auditing books or settling accounts, Seth, but I also know that I have a sort of knack for these kinds of things. There were holes here and there that I just couldn't account for. This concerns me because I have so much to learn and so much to catch up on, but I still have a feeling there is something amiss here. I hope though that when we go back into them tomorrow I will feel better about everything and will be able to understand some of the discrepancies.

Thank you, Seth, for letting me get some of my concerns off of my mind for I certainly wouldn't want to put any burden on you. But I felt I needed a sounding board and you were the first and only one who came to my mind.

Now, let me tell you some good news!

As I have told you, Grandfather is improving daily. Mrs. King is so dedicated to making him healthy again. She makes him laugh and eat his meals just as he should, or otherwise he would have to answer to her! And you know, of course, about

Doctor Patrick. He is not only Grandfather's doctor, but one of his dearest friends. He comes by and checks on him several times a week. He has also told me that I should be alert when visitors enter the house, which doesn't exactly make me comfortable, but I know under the circumstances, that it is wise advice.

So enough of my ramblings and on to something much happier!

Now I believe, though they have not declared this yet, that Doctor Patrick and Molly are very much in Love! They have been out to several functions together and seem to be so well-suited to each other. Both are Irish and, in fact, could be brother and sister they resemble each other so much. And when he leaves the house after talking with Grandfather and checking him health wise, it is Molly who rises to see him to the door, with a little bit of a blush rising on her cheeks....

Mother keeps me up on the news of home, and I am so happy that our Banks are still as bright, sunshiny and beautiful as I remember them. I am homesick, as I am sure you can tell from this letter, and I hope it won't be long until I am on that boat headed back to the beautiful shores of North Carolina.

I cannot wait to see our Anna Catharine. I am so honored to know they gave her a part of my name! Just another treat that awaits me. Leave some spoiling for me to indulge in just a little bit. Give your Mother and Father my love.

I am sorry to have bent your ear with my problems, but I thank you anyway and I feel better just to have written and put my thoughts on paper.

As I am sure you know, I miss you.

Your dearest friend,

Catharine

THE BLACK PELICAN

PART IV

CHAPTER 13

(Seth's Response)

Well, Seth read this letter and reread it, and then he read it again. He needed to be sure he was not reading into it more than Catharine intended. He was sure, however, that she was in need of a helping hand to deal with these problems, or in the least, she needed to be able to discuss them with someone.

And he decided right there on the spot that he himself was that person she needed!

Hadn't she told him so in the letter when she said, "she needed to talk with someone she *did* and *could* utterly trust." Weren't those her words? Without directly saying it, she had told him that she needed him there to help her. She needed a confidant and she had chosen him to be that confidant!

Besides, they needed to be together during this stressful time. His hope was that soon they would be together forever and now was the time to let her know that. He was going to tell her that he wanted to be there for her forever and he was going to give her the opportunity to say that she wanted to be with him forever also.

Well, he had a decision to make. Was he ready to commit right here and now? Yes he was, he said to himself, and with that he made the most important decision he had ever made!

The first move he had to make was to pay Catharine's mother and father a visit. He knew what he had to do and he was now ready to do it. When Mrs. Chase answered the door she greeted Seth warmly with a hug. "To what in the world do we owe this pleasure this morning, Seth!" They were always happy when Seth dropped by.

Seth told her that he had something he would like to discuss with her and Mr. Chase. At that minute Mr. Chase, having heard them talking from the kitchen where he was having a second cup of coffee, arrived at the door too and greeted Seth with a big slap on the back. Seth asked if he could talk with them and, of course they agreed. Mr. Chase joins them, coffee in hand, and Mrs. Chase asked Seth if she could get him a cup of coffee also. Seth suddenly felt that a good, strong cup of coffee might be just what he needed to help him through this! They knew something important was on Seth's mind because of the serious look on his face and the tone of his voice.

They all sat down together and allowed Seth time to collect

his thoughts. As he started talking, Seth developed a grin across his entire face. Mr. and Mrs. Chase looked at each other with an expression of total confusion, and then Seth began to speak.

"Mr. and Mrs. Chase, I have something very important I would like to ask of you and it concerns me and Catharine. I have loved Catharine probably since the first time I ever saw her. I believe she may feel the same way about me, though we have not discussed this. I have just decided that I would like to take a trip to London to visit with her and to offer any help that I can give her while I am there. I know she has a lot of decisions to make right now and I feel like maybe she could use, and would like to have, an extra hand right now. But mainly, I would like to ask for her hand in marriage. However, I would not do this without the permission and blessing from both of you."

Well, this news was received with such joy, laughter and excitement. They both told Seth that they had always thought of him as a son, and now he would be, in fact, a son! They told him that their ultimate hope for Catharine had always been that she would find the perfect mate for her life and now that seemed to be a hope that would come true.

Of course, Catharine would have to agree to all of this first! They all laughed and agreed that it would be a grand idea to at least discuss it with her!

Seth told them that a while back he had been asked by a representative of one of the boat building companies in London if he would be interested in visiting their company. They were interested in some of his ideas which were new to them and he, in turn, was interested in some techniques they used which he believed might be beneficial to his own company here in the Outer Banks. Therefore, he felt the trip could also turn out to be a wise business decision for him.

Seth told them he was going to make arrangements immediately for the journey and he would keep them informed of every development. However, he told them he would like for the visit to be a surprise for Catharine, so he would appreciate it if they would keep his secret. They both agreed. They also told Seth that they were so happy that he was going to London to be with Catharine because they had been concerned about all of the decisions she was having to make by herself. They told Seth that he didn't realize what a relief this decision had brought to them and for that they thanked him again and told him that they believed they would now be able to sleep better at night.

The next move for Seth would be to talk with his mother and father and tell them of his plans. He knew they would be happy for him for they had always loved Catharine, and he was right.

They were so supportive of all of his plans and said he only had to ask for any help he needed. His father told him he would arrange for his lifesaving station duties to be covered and that he himself would take care of the boat building business.

His mother agreed to pack his personal needs but she gave

him some much needed additional advice, which he had not yet thought of, and told him that he should visit one of the good tailors in London and purchase some lovely suits, shirts, shoes and accessories. "You know," she said, "You will want to impress Catharine and let her know you can dress *citified* too!" At this, Seth laughed, but he thought at the same time that his mother had a good point. He decided right then that before he saw Catharine in London he would be outfitted by a fine London tailor.

He was on a mission, in fact, he was on several missions! Seth was getting into the spirit of things and found that he was enjoying it all. His spirits were soaring, like the Black Pelican, because he could feel himself getting closer and closer to his Catharine.

When Catharine awoke the next morning, she was exhausted. She had spent the night thinking of recent events that were disturbing and even frightening. She was happy, however, that she had written the letter to Seth in which she shared her fears and concerns with him.

She and Molly had breakfast, as usual, with Grandfather Chase. Under the watchful eye of Mrs. King, he ate a good breakfast and then said he wanted to talk privately with Catharine. When he said this Catharine looked at Mrs. King, because she knew Mrs. King had orders from Doctor Patrick that he was to be left alone with no one. However, Mrs. King prepared to leave the room with Molly and told him that she would be right outside the door.

CHAPTER 14

(Catharine Meets Mr. Spencer)

When they were alone, Grandfather asked Catharine if she were feeling alright to which she answered that she was. He said he thought she had looked very tired for a few days. Was she homesick? Did she think she needed to see Doctor Patrick for a good checkup? She thanked him for keeping such an alert eye on her but assured him that she was fine. Maybe just a little bit home-sick, but she was looking forward now to diving into learning the ins and outs of the business. Also, that she had sat in with Jake Parks yesterday morning, and she was meeting him this morning to continue their work. Grandfather told her that he did not want her to get overtired and not to try to learn everything too fast.

He also said he would call in one of his oldest business col-leagues, a Mr. Spencer, to help her if she would feel more comfort-able with this setup. She agreed that maybe that would be a good thing and they agreed that she would work in the mornings with Jake and in the afternoons with Mr. Spencer. That way Jake would not have to be there all day every day because, as Grandfather said, he was sure Jake had other clients he needed to be with and Catharine could feel free to take as much time to acquaint herself with every phase of the business as she needed.

However Jake, when he learned the proposed new setup from Grandfather, was not in the least happy. He argued that the two men would not have the same ways of keeping their records and that it would be confusing to Catharine. But Grandfather insisted saying that the differences would keep them more alert and should even make the learning more interesting. Jake could see Grandfather had made up his mind and he knew him well enough to know that when he had made up his mind you needed to leave it alone.

As Catharine and Jake plowed over page after page of facts and figures she realized that he skipped certain areas and said they would come back to them. Catharine made mental pictures of those pages thinking that she and Mr. Spencer would go over them later, and so the plan was developed in her mind that the ones Jake skipped over would be the very ones that they would come back to in the afternoons.

In a week's time, there was no doubt in Catharine's or Mr. Spencer's mind that Grandfather's books had been tampered with. At the same time it was revealed to both of them that they were dealing with a huge amount of embezzlement, and they felt they knew the embezzler! But they had to handle this all very carefully because they knew they were dealing with a thief and they had no idea how far he would go to keep from getting caught. Catharine also thought about the poison found in Grandfather's blood work and if this, in fact, were all connected, she felt sure he was capable even of murder! She was smart enough to know they had to be very careful....

That night when Doctor Patrick came by to check on Grandfather, Catharine asked to talk with him again. She told him all about what she and Mr. Spencer had found and the evidence was indisputable that there was a large amount of embezzlement involved.

She was at a loss as to which way was the best way to proceed because she was afraid of what he might do next. Mr. Spencer had suggested to her that she needed to get Scotland Yard involved and she needed to do it now. She knew for a fact that it would have to be confronted soon. She was becoming frightened for their whole household, for which she felt responsible, and now with Grandfather being ill, she was indeed responsible!

Doctor Patrick told her about a friend of his, Detective Casey, who was a detective at Scotland Yard. He would contact him tonight, if Catharine thought it wise, tell him the whole story, and ask him for his department's help. Doctor Patrick felt they needed professional help right now because he felt this very possibly had developed into a dangerous situation.

He said he would be back in touch with Catharine in the morning, and told her to be very careful if she had to deal with

Jake in the meantime. He also told her not to indicate in any way that she felt there was something amiss. He even went so far as to tell Catharine he would ask his detective friend to have someone discreetly guard the house tonight. Then, by tomorrow, they would be in the process of making an overall plan.

Another night of tossing and turning. It seemed like this was the new order of things in Catharine's life. She felt so responsible for those under her roof and to think of any one of them being in danger was a heavy load for her to shoulder alone.

She tried to focus on the sights and sounds of home. She pictured the laughing gulls, the gentle splashing of the waves, the beautiful sunset colors.... She was missing the calmness and serenity of her beloved Outer Banks!

And while focusing on the beautiful beach with the water of the Atlantic lapping at her feet, she even imagined that she saw the dolphins playing right offshore. She could feel her loved ones near, and combined with familiar sights and sounds that she loved, she felt safe and protected. There she was near her Mother and Father, and Seth! And finally she was transported to that peaceful and much missed place and she fell asleep.

CHAPTER 15

(Jake's Downfall)

This morning the house was a beehive of activity. Catharine and Molly were on their way to Grandfather's room for their daily morning visit and breakfast. Catharine was not going to meet with Jake this morning, because he had another appointment. This worked out perfectly for Catharine because she was meeting with the Scotland Yard detective, Inspector Casey, and Doctor Patrick at Doctor Patrick's office.

Inspector Casey was a big and burly Irishman and Catharine immediately felt at ease with him. In fact, his manner was so relaxed and his happy demeanor was such that Catharine wondered if he was going to be the person she needed to help her with this serious situation that by now had her at her wit's end. However, after pleasantries had been exchanged and after the situation, as they knew it, had been related to him, he became a totally different man. He was immediately totally focused, dedicated to business and the tasks at hand.

He asked question after question concerning Jake Parks. He asked her to remember even the smallest details, and to try and remember every single thing she had ever known or heard about him. Questions arose about how he first became acquainted with her Grandfather, just how he came to be hired in the first place and how he had become so totally trusted that his decisions were never questioned.

Catharine answered all of his questions as well as she knew how, and the answers that she didn't know she agreed she would find for him as soon as possible. Actually, she was not at all sure how all of this had come about. She knew that Jake had come on the scene around the time Grandfather got sick. He had written to her about the fine young man he had come to depend on so much and how he didn't know what he would do without him.

Catharine could only think that Jake was probably already putting something poisonous in Grandfather's food or drink and that he was probably already doctoring her Grandfather's books. It made her sad that someone he had come to trust and depended on so much would end up being such a miserable person.

While Catharine thought about Jake and how he had become so deeply engrained into their household, it dawned on her that it seemed no one knew anything about Jake's personal life. She had never heard Jake or Grandfather mention a family member, where Jake was raised, or any type of information concerning his past. She must ask Grandfather. Surely they had talked of such things at some point while their business relationship and their friendship grew?

Catharine's thoughts returned to Detective Casey who was outlining the strategy they would develop to, most importantly, ensure the safety of the household. At the same time, their actions would need to be as inconspicuous as possible so as not to bring attention to any parts of their plan.

Detective Casey said that he had planted an employee of Scotland Yard as a new maid and that she would be on the job this afternoon. Catharine was told to let Mrs. King know about this in order for the both of them to be able to work together should the need occur.

He told Catharine that she would be protected at all times in ways that she wouldn't even know about and this did a lot to improve her confidence because she was beginning to feel very overcome by the entire situation. Inspector Casey also told Catharine that she may from time to time notice a new face mingling with the staff that she did not recognize, but not to worry about it because they would have been put there by Scotland Yard for the whole household's protection, to be on lookout and to take notice of anything out of the ordinary.

It was also suggested by Detective Casey that Grandfather Chase be told about the suspicions regarding Jake. He felt it was better for him to find out sooner rather than later, because now things were swirling too fast for it to be kept from him much longer anyway.

Detective Casey told each of them to call him immediately when anything looked out of the ordinary. If it turned out to be of no importance, then good. But sometimes even the smallest of things can be of great importance in the overall scheme of things. Then with some stern warnings regarding their safety, and also assurances that they were all well protected, he told them goodbye and said he would be in touch tomorrow.

Catharine chose her words very carefully when she told Grandfather the story of Jake's infidelity. But there was no sugar-coating the basic story, Jake had definitely stolen from him and he was also suspected of other crimes against him. Grandfather Chase had depended on him totally before Catharine and Molly had arrived and had never once suspected him of any wrongdoing. He had trusted him implicitly. However, he had to say that he had not been able to keep a watchful eye on his businesses during that time, which was not like him, but according to the evidence as it stood now, Jake had abused the power and trust Grandfather had bestowed upon him.

When Catharine left him, Grandfather Chase was staring in disbelief trying to take all of this in and trying to make some sense of it.

Again, he was so thankful that Catharine was there and that she had taken it upon herself to call upon Mr. Spencer, his old friend and business partner, for help and guidance. This proved to him once again what a good head she had for business and that his decision to leave all of his assets to her had been a wise one.

That night Catharine and Molly had dinner with Grandfather Chase in the dining room. He was feeling so well that he wanted them all to gather together at the table. They also invited Doctor Patrick to join them and they enjoyed a delicious meal and did not mention Jake at all during dinner.

However, afterwards they all felt the air needed to be cleared and they each needed to share with Grandfather everything they knew about Jake and his disloyalty to them all. They each told all they knew about how he had seized the opportunity to take advantage of Grandfather's health situation by taking money from different accounts. Then, they also told him the thing that made him sadder than anything else and that was when they told him of their suspicions that Jake had been poisoning his food or drink and that his whole life threatening situation may have been caused by Jake and his greediness.

This was the part that was hardest for Grandfather to hear because he truly thought that Jake cared for him.

They also told him about Scotland Yard's involvement and the people Inspector Casey had placed in the household for their protection. Grandfather immediately asked for a meeting with the Inspector to be set up as soon as possible. His mind was totally sound and he was getting stronger daily. Further, he demanded that he be kept informed about everything that had or would develop. They were amazed that instead of bringing him down, he seemed to be energized by the situations confronting them. In addition, he wanted to be in control of the situation and not someone they would inform once a decision had been made. This sounded like the Grandfather that she knew and loved!

It made Catharine happy to see her Grandfather returning once again to the take-charge person he had always been. He was never the one to be informed once a decision had been made, but he was the one that made the decision in the first place. Thinking back on her memories of her father's relationship with Grandfather Chase, wasn't that exactly what he had said? Didn't he always want a voice in decisions, but never got one? Some things never change and, for once, she was happy to see her Grandfather's old form returning.

Soon though, they decided they should get some rest because who knew what tomorrow would bring. Grandfather bid all a goodnight and headed off to bed with his nighttime nurse close by his side. However, Catharine, Molly and Doctor Patrick sat and talked for some time. They needed some time to relax before retiring tonight.

This had been another stressful day for this entire household.

As they talked, Doctor Patrick asked Catharine to share with him some of her memories of the Outer Banks. Of course, she was instantly ready to talk about the "Banks." And Molly was right in there with her memories and her own set of stories. They talked about how different the Atlantic Ocean looked there. How the skies were almost constantly blue with nary a cloud in the sky. The temperatures were most always mild, even in the dead of winter. Why you could stroll on the beach most all year long there, of course at times you needed a jacket and a hood to protect you from the winds.

In fact, these were some of Catharine's favorite times to walk beside the ocean and feel the fresh air that made you feel so alert and alive! And she loved to pick up the beautiful shells and sea glass that she found in lovely colors which washed in from who knows where onto the shore. She collected this faithfully and displayed it in jars in her room, where she now had an amazing collection.

The children loved playing in the waters by the sea and during their summer vacation from school you could expect to find most every child who lived on the "Banks" playing there after they had finished their chores.

She told him about the slow paced life there where every-one shared the bounty of the land, but also shared its harshness. Catharine let him know that even though it was her favorite place on earth, life was not without its hardships there. Life there though, was much simpler and these simple pleasures were what made these people most happy.

She noticed that Patrick was totally absorbed in her revelations about her beloved home. Mostly Molly just nodded agreement and smiled and Patrick was smitten by their love of this little strip of an island that they called home. In fact, it was at that time that Patrick and Molly broke a huge bit of news to Catharine!

Molly was glowing when she spoke. "Catharine," she said, "Patrick has asked me to marry him and I have accepted!" There was such a celebration between the three of them. They hugged, they cried, they laughed, they were happy! What better thing to think on after this week of sadness than to plan for an upcoming wedding! This was just what they all needed, something entirely happy!

When will the big day be? Where will the wedding be?

"Whoa," Patrick laughed, "Another question before we answer the one before it!"

Catharine knew she was asking the questions too fast, but she was so excited. She agreed to be still and wait for the answers, but it was very hard.

"Well," Patrick replied, "This brings us to the rest of the big news. We have decided we want to relocate to the Outer Banks of North Carolina. We would like to be married there and I would like to open my medical practice there. Molly says there is ample opportunity for a new doctor there and that she believes I would be well received.

Frankly, I have become so excited about this island just listening to the two of you that I cannot wait to become a part of it. Of course, we will postpone everything until our affairs here are straightened out.

I would never leave Grandfather Chase until all is resolved, but Molly and I felt we had to announce our intentions or bust, and we also feel it will be a much-needed vent of happiness for all of us. Molly said she had written her mother and father announcing their plans, but they had not had time to respond to her letter yet.

Of course, she and Patrick had discussed where they would be married, in their special little church, with Father Sam officiating. There would be a simple reception, which Molly's mother would host, because that's the way it was done in the "Banks", simply, with much love, with everyone participating, each in his own way.

But Molly did ask Catharine that very night if she would be her Maid of Honor. Catharine cried again and said emphatically that she would be more than honored. Patrick asked if Catharine thought Seth would agree to be his best man, since Patrick's own father was not living. He already felt that Seth, although they had not officially met, was someone he would come to know as a close friend when they moved to the Outer Banks.

After Patrick said goodnight and left, Catharine and Molly sat and talked for a long time. They reminisced about their special times together and both decided they were good and homesick for the Banks and family and friends. They talked about what kind of gown Molly would make for her wedding and what kind of gown Catharine would wear as her maid of honor. They both hoped the problems here in London would be resolved soon so they could start making wedding plans and plans to go home!

Catharine yawned, Molly too, they hugged and decided they had had enough excitement for one day. Soon they were snug in their beds, thinking happy thoughts, and drifting lazily into a sweet, dreamless sleep.

Little did they know their house was about to be fearfully awakened. Catharine and Molly had both drifted off into a deep sleep when a series of loud noises awoke them both.

CHAPTER 16

(A House In Lockdown)

They put on their robes as fast as they possibly could and ran into each other in the hallway outside their rooms. Molly was the first to ask what in the world was happening. Catharine replied that she had no idea, but they found themselves running toward the stairway leading downstairs hoping to discover the reason for the confusion. As they came to the top of the stairs they were immediately stopped by one of the detectives from Scotland Yard who told them to go back into their rooms, or possibly both should go into the same room and lock the door. They were told not to come out until they were given the word that all was clear and that it was safe for them to do so.

Catharine asked what was happening and the detective only told her that there was an intruder in the house. He told her that the Department had everything under control, but their job right now was to make sure everyone in the house was kept safe.

She asked if her Grandfather was safe and the detective told her that he was indeed safe and locked in his room with a detective, his nurse and William, Mr. Chase's butler. He told her that Inspector Casey had specifically told him to relay the message to Catharine that her Grandfather was safe. He also wanted him to tell her that the situation was under control and that she and Molly need not be afraid because they were being protected by London's best!

Both girls were frightened and they both went back into Catharine's room to await further instructions from the detective. They were frightened, but they also had great faith in all of the people who were there to help them. Still there is a certain amount of fear that you just have to deal with when the safety of the people you love is at stake.

She and Molly then talked about just who would break into their home in the middle of the night and for what reason. One person at once came to their minds. Jake Parks!

That was when they heard the inspector's loud shout, "Stop or I will fire!" It was then they heard a shot ring out through the house. Confused voices mingled with loud noises which sounded like running or of an ongoing struggle. Then things quieted. They heard someone yell, "He is bleeding badly. Get an ambulance here as soon as possible."

Neither Catharine nor Molly had any idea who had been shot. It was almost impossible for them to remain locked in Catharine's room not knowing anything about this entire situation, but they both knew there was danger lurking out there and the inspector had asked them to stay there for their own safety.

They sat there for a long time it seemed before they heard the ambulance's arrival. There was confusion again as they prepared whoever the patient was for transport. They watched out of the bedroom window as they loaded this person into the ambulance, but they were covered by a blanket which made it impossible to recognize the patient.

Shortly after the ambulance left their home, there was a knock on the door and a voice that Catharine recognized as the inspector's. He told them they could unlock the door now and that the danger was over. They were never more glad to see anyone.

He was like a tower of strength who had been there to protect them all the time and they both wept for joy when they saw him. "I am so sorry that you young ladies had to endure this tonight," he said. "Please know that we believe all of this will soon be over and you can go back to living your life as before." Catharine laughed at this and said she doubted if that would ever happen again, to which he replied, "Yes, you will be able to return to your happy lives again, but I will say that it probably will take some time."

Catharine then asked if they knew who the intruder was and the inspector replied with the answer she knew she would hear. He said it was Jake Parks. He was discovered in the house by a maid who was placed there by Scotland Yard. Her job was solely to keep an eye out for any movement she saw in the house by anyone not authorized to be there and to report it immediately. She was making her rounds through the house and fortunately saw Jake coming out of Mr. Chase's office with several books containing business records and ledgers for the past several years.

Our people were stationed outside. Her job then was to make sure everyone inside the house was locked inside their rooms safe from the intruder, because at that time we didn't know for sure who the intruder was. Then, our detectives who are trained daily for crimes such as this, confronted him. He was armed and when I ordered him to stop or I would shoot, he started to pull his gun from his holster. That was when I did what I don't like to do, but sometimes I have to do, sorrowfully, I shot him.

Molly and Catharine then asked at the same time if Jake was still alive. Inspector Casey replied that he was still alive and was being transported to the hospital. He would go there and check on his condition after he made completely sure all was well here. His people would remain here until they were sure that any danger had passed.

He asked if there was anything more he could do for either of them before he left for the hospital. Neither of them could think of anything further, but asked that he let them know about Jake's condition when he found out and they thanked him for his protection and care throughout this sorrowful ordeal.

The next thing on Catharine's mind was Grandfather. She and Molly quickly got themselves ready for their morning visit with him. They all knew this would be a different morning visit than they had ever had with him. Grandfather was genuinely fond of Jake and until recently had considered him as a close friend and part of his family.

What could he have done to change this sad outcome? Could he have paid him more? These were just some of the questions Grandfather Chase was asking himself. Grandfather believed he paid Jake a very generous salary. He had also given him many gifts unrelated to salary, just because he considered him a young man that he liked, trusted and that he wanted to see succeed!

What a jewel Mrs. King was. When they got to Grandfather's room, Mrs. King had him engaged in a serious game of chess. In fact, they were discussing the possible fact that one of them had made an illegal move. And on purpose, to make it worse.

After feeling certain that Mrs. King had everything under control, they decided to prepare themselves for what would most assuredly be an eventful day. When Catharine and Molly came back into Catharine's room, they talked about all of these things. Grandfather said he wanted to be updated on Jake's condition and with anything that would ultimately indicate what was to become of him. They told him that all of that was out of his hands now and in the hands of the law, but they would make sure he knew of all developments regarding his case.

When Inspector Casey arrived at the hospital he asked to see Jake Parks. There was police presence all around, due to the nature of this patient's injuries, and the inspector was immediately put in touch with the nurse attending to Jake. He was also informed that the doctor who had taken the bullet from Jake had surely, thus far anyway, been credited with saving Jake's life and he was none other than Doctor Patrick Kelly. The nurse told him, however, that Jake's condition was very critical and that there was little hope that he would survive.

Inspector Casey asked if he was conscious and his nurse said he was coming in and out of consciousness. He asked if he could visit with him, even though he knew his condition was very serious, there were some questions that he needed to ask Jake. He told the nurse that if Jake wasn't allowed to answer these questions they might never know the answers and, as in any investigation it was vital to the case to know as many of the facts as possible. The nurse agreed and led Inspector Casey to Jake's room.

Jake lay very still in his bed. At first, Inspector Casey thought he might have already died he was so still. However, just then he noticed a slight movement of Jake's right hand. He walked over to his bed and asked, "Jake, can you hear me?" Jake made no response for a short time but then opened his eyes and looked at the inspector with a questioning glance. Inspector Casey identified himself and Jake's demeanor seemed to slightly change. Jake seemed to have gained purpose because he took a deep breath and without being asked started to tell the inspector the story that needed to be told.

Jake said Mr. Chase had been so good to him. He had been fair always, but when he made Catharine the heir of his estate, he knew his days were limited where he had a free hand in Mr. Chase's affairs. He knew his time to become unimaginably wealthy was drawing to a close, and this had always driven him; he wanted to be very wealthy.

It was then that the thought entered his mind to give Mr. Chase the medication that would very slowly cause him to lose control of his body and mind. That would give him unlimited time in his office and the opportunity to make changes to certain business deals, which would never be discovered because he had no idea that Catharine would be as astute concerning business as she was. However, he knew on the day that she came into the office to go over the books with him, that he was in trouble. She was not just a "woman" who had taken over Mr. Chase's affairs, but an intelligent businesswoman!

The books he was taking from the house when he was caught were ones containing the changes he had made to the accounts. He felt that if he could dispose of these books, he could find a way out of this damning situation. But he had no idea that Scotland Yard was already on the case, let alone that agents were stationed at that very moment on the inside of Mr. Chase's home. He was caught completely off guard when they made their presence known.

Jake closed his eyes as if he were suddenly too tired to open them. The inspector let him rest and in a minute or two

Jake seemed to come awake and he went on saying, "Would you deliver a message to Mr. Chase for me? Would you please tell him how much I regret what I did. He was the kindest person that I ever knew. I hate that I repaid his kindnesses in such a way. He certainly did not deserve any of this. Please ask him to forgive me. Tell him for me that I am truly sorry."

He went on talking about how he could have been a wealthy man in London even without doing these shameful things. He pondered on how these things were so clearly shameful to him now, but had seemed to be a sure path to success and riches when he started this game that had caused him to lose everything. He talked about his life before he met Mr. Chase and how he had helped him to get started in business. That Mr. Chase was wholly responsible for his successful start in the business world as he was not from a wealthy family and had no connections of his own that would ever help him attain such a start. However, success and wealth were what he had aspired to all of his life. He told the inspector that Mr. Chase had introduced him to friends and business connections in order for him to get a smooth start in his career.

He seemed to have little energy left, but he said he wanted the inspector to also give Catharine a message from him. Jake asked him to ask her for her forgiveness also. He asked the inspector to tell her that he was so sorry that he caused her so much grief concerning her Grandfather. And that Mr. Chase was blessed to have a granddaughter who loved him so much.

Then, Jake closed his eyes for the last time and died.

CHAPTER 17

(A Time to Move On)

Inspector Casey was glad he was here with Jake. Even people who had made very bad mistakes in their lives shouldn't die alone.

Inspector Casey had collected all of the information he needed to know, but he sat for a while beside Jake's body and thought of the sad ending to this young man's life. He wished Jake had been able to be satisfied with the many advantages laid before him, but that was not the case. The inspector also looked back on his part in Jake's death and it hurt his heart to think that he had taken this young man's life. Any way he looked at it, he could have done no differently, but it still made him sad. That was the part he didn't like about his job.

Finally he knew it was time for him to continue to complete the tasks his job called for and that was to deliver Jake's messages to Mr. Chase and Catharine, and so he got up and left the hospital.

He soon arrived at the Chase residence where the family and staff were all gathered together trying to get a picture of all that had gone on the night before. They all knew Jake well because he had been a frequent visitor in this house for several years and they saw him as a likable and handsome young man with such a promising future in front of him. Little did they know....

It served the inspector well that they all were gathered together because he felt they all deserved to know the basic truths of the case. He told them first that Jake had not made it and that he was dead. He said to them that he was sorry that things could not have ended differently but that Jake would have faced many years in prison for what would most surely be a charge of attempted murder and more years still for the charge of embezzlement. Then he asked to speak privately with Mr. Chase and Catharine. The staff left the room and resumed their individual duties, which they were glad to do. They would be happy to return to their normal routines.

Inspector Casey, Grandfather and Catharine gathered in Grandfather Chase's room where they made themselves comfortable and started what they knew would be a sad discussion.

They each were served a cup of tea with several familiar scone, cookie and muffin type tea treats which they enjoyed for several minutes.

Then, the inspector knew it was time to get down to what Mr. Chase and Catharine were waiting to hear, which were the details of Jake's death and anything new the inspector had uncovered about the case. First he told Mr. Chase about Jake's apologies to him and how sorry he was that he had not taken advantage of the many good opportunities that Mr. Chase put before him. He told him how much he respected him for his kindnesses to him and how sad that he realized it all too late.

He also told Catharine how he knew that he would be found out when the two of them went over the books on that first day. He knew then that she was not the average woman who really didn't know or care much for business matters. She, he knew, understood and would bring him down. The inspector said he felt Jake was genuine when he apologized to them both for his actions and asked for their forgiveness.

Both Grandfather and Catharine agreed that they were sorry for Jake. They wished they had known some way to help him before things went as far as they did. What a shame, they thought, for him to have so many opportunities before him and not be able to be happy or to take advantage of them. It was sad that he always wanted more. They would have liked to have been able to make a difference, but it was not to be for Jake. Their hearts were sad....

THE BLACK PELICAN

PART V

CHAPTER 18

(The Visitor)

The next morning the doorbell rang and William was prompt, as usual, to answer. When he opened the door there was an unfamiliar handsome young man there. William asked if he could help him and the young man said, "My name is Seth, I am here to see Catharine, will you tell her I am here?"

Seth also said, "I would appreciate it if you would not tell her my name because she doesn't know that I am in London. You see, I have traveled from our home in the Outer Banks of America to see her and I would like for this to be somewhat of a surprise." William smiled broadly and said very properly, "Certainly, Sir, I have heard your name mentioned many times and I am sure Miss Catharine will be delighted to know that you are here!"

Catharine and Molly were having breakfast with Grandfather in his room when William announced that Catharine had a visitor. Catharine couldn't imagine who it could be this early in the morning. She also thought it quite unusual that William had not inquired as to their name. Quite unusual....

However, nothing had been usual about this week so far and she thought no more about it until....

"Seth"!
"Oh my goodness!"
"Is that really you!"
"What in the world are you doing here?"
"Am I losing my mind!"
"Am I seeing things?"

Along with several more exclamations, then immediately she was in Seth's arms. She had never been there before, but without hesitation she sailed into his open arms! "Let's don't talk. I am afraid you will just up and disappear and we will break this wonderful spell." Then it was Seth's turn to speak and he said, "Catharine, I will not disappear. I will be here with you until you are able to return home with me. I have come for you! I love you! I am asking you to marry me! I have already asked for and received your Mother and Father's blessings. So, first I will ask you for your answer. Will you marry me?"

"Seth, Well, of course I will marry you!"
"I have always loved you!"
"I have needed you here with me so much you wouldn't believe it!"
"Thank you for coming to me, to help me!"

"Oh, Seth, please don't disappear, please don't go until I can go with you!"

"Catharine," Seth said, "I will not leave London without you! Never! You never have to fear that we will be apart again!"

"Oh Seth," Catharine said, "My heart is bursting with joy, all of this has been so overwhelming. I have so much to tell you about what has been going on here. I have felt like I have been trying to take care of a huge sinking ship with no one to help me. Are you sure you can stay here and help me make these decisions? I am dealing with so many things that you don't even know of yet, but if you can stay with me and will help me I feel so much more confident that together we will be able to make right choices and decisions." Then she said....

"But first, before we talk anymore about things here, I want you to tell me about home, about all those in the Outer Banks that I love and miss so much. Seth, I have been so homesick for all of you. I have longed for the serenity of those beautiful waters and those sandy beaches. I have longed to stroll along them and look for the sea treasures I find there and the peace and serenity of it all. As you can see, there is much more luxury here, but I can assure you it is all very costly. Here there is none of that quality of life that I have come to love. I miss our friends coming in and out, people of all walks of life living together almost as one big family. I miss that caring and taking care of each other attitude that is there. So, Seth, tell me about home...."

They had moved into the main parlor by that time, and William came to the door, knocked, and asked if he could do anything for them or would they like some refreshments. Catharine then introduced Seth to William, and she told William that tea would be nice. She also asked him to let the others know that it was Seth who was here and that she and Seth wanted to be alone for just a little while to visit. William assured her he would convey the message and would return shortly with their tea.

Seth walked over to Catharine and held out his arms and she walked into them as though it was the most natural thing in the world. They, neither of them, were embarrassed by their open expressions of love and the joy they were experiencing for the first time in their lives. For a while they just stood there, quiet, in each other's arms.

Finally, Seth smiled and said he supposed that he should get on with telling her the news from home or the day would be gone and he would have to return to his hotel. Catharine let him know that Grandfather would never allow a visitor to his home from America to stay at a hotel. She knew he would insist that Seth move from the hotel to the empty apartment next to his. Which made Catharine's heart so happy to know that tonight Seth would sleep here and they would be under the same roof. She could already feel a soothing feeling come over her and she knew that tonight she would feel safe again.

Seth told her about every small bit of news that he could think of and about the people he knew she loved. He told her how they all missed her and they all sent their love.

She asked if they realized he was coming to ask her to marry him (she blushed at voicing that out loud) and he said he believed they probably did. He told her that he was not too good at keeping a secret where she was concerned and he thought they read between the lines how he felt about her. But, he told her they had no way of knowing if the feelings were mutual. So they will be waiting with bated breath to hear her answer and to see how everything works out.

Father Sam sent his love to her and said for her to hurry home. That he missed her playing the piano, but she had several students who were coming along and they were practicing harder than usual because they loved the compliments they got and wanted to play well to impress Catharine when she returned home. Also, her father had been known to bring his fiddle a time or two and play some of his old-time gospel tunes, which the whole community loved.

Her dad had decided to build on to his store again but wanted to talk with Molly before he made the final plans to see if she would be interested in renting a portion of it to open a shop for her sewing business. There she could sell women's, men's and children's articles of clothing and handle miscellaneous sewing needs. She could even make dresses or whatever she wanted in advance, like they do in some big cities, and she might also want to have a window where she could display them? She could make changes as she wanted. Both Seth and Catharine thought this idea would really please Molly. Catharine didn't tell Seth at this point that Patrick had asked Molly to marry him. She thought she would wait until he finished telling her the news from home before she started in on her news from here.

Of course, his favorite bit of news concerned his new niece, Anna Catharine! He declared her to be the best and most beautiful baby ever born and that he was absolutely her favorite person. In fact, he said that she even looked like him! She smiled right on cue and almost always slept through the night now. This, of course, he had only heard tell of because he, himself, was always sound asleep at those times and in another house even. So when they spoke of her sleeping through the night more often now, he couldn't possibly know about the sleepless nights Sarah and Abe endured to get her to this point! But she is the high point of everyone in the neighborhood's day. Even Father Sam is totally smitten by her and visits Sarah and Abe's home much more often these days. So Anna Catharine even had some extra prayers going up for her and, as Seth said, you can never have too many of those!

Seth told her every bit of news he could think of about the young and old folks that they both loved. He told her that there hadn't been any bad storms as of yet this summer. Maybe they would have a quiet hurricane season on the Outer Banks this year. But now, he said he wanted to know all about London. How her Grandfather was progressing, about Molly, and all about Jake. Of course, Seth didn't know at that point that Jake was dead, and so Catharine began to tell him about all the things that had happened in the short time she had been here. Where to start....

She told him that Grandfather was so very much improved. No one could believe this was the same old Grandfather who was almost dead when she got here. He was walking now, enjoying his meals and his company. He and Mrs. King had become great friends and had found out that they both were serious chess players. And serious they were! Sometimes you could hear them arguing outside Grandfather's room about a certain move one or the other had made. Catharine's face lit up as she talked on about his improved health and mental state. She felt like her old Grandfather had returned.

Then she told Seth about Doctor Patrick. How he had been so dedicated to all of them and to her Grandfather. He was such a comfort to them during those unsettling times of not knowing what to expect from one day to the next regarding Grandfather's health.

Then, when the tests revealed that there was a poisonous substance in his blood, they all were in a panic. Doctor Patrick let them all know in no uncertain terms that something dangerous was going on here and he was instrumental in putting the necessary precautions into place. He was even the one who had brought Scotland Yard onto the case, and at just the right time because Jake was beginning to feel trapped by now and he knew that most probably it was only a matter of time before he would be found out.

Next she explained to Seth how they found that Jake was responsible for Grandfather's illness. That he had slowly been poisoning his food which gave Jake more time to spend in Grandfather's office altering his books and, ultimately, stealing from him.

She told Seth then about Jake's death. She told him about Scotland Yard planting their detectives throughout the house for their protection. How they blended with the staff in such a way that they would never be noticed.

She told him about Detective Casey who had protected them in ways they never knew of until after it was all over.

She explained to him about hearing the confusion downstairs on the night Jake was shot. That she and Molly came out into the hall outside their room, but were immediately told to go back into their rooms and lock the door until they were told it was safe to open them. They both decided to go back into Catharine's room so they could at least be together. At that point, she told Seth, they didn't realize it was Jake who was in the house, that she heard Detective Casey order him to stop, which he did not do, and then she heard the shot. An ambulance was called, and it seemed the confusion stopped.

After Jake had been taken off in the ambulance, Detective Casey came up and told them they could open the door. He explained that it was Jake who had entered the house and he had several of Grandfather's ledger books that he was trying to take out of the house. These were, no doubt, books that he knew contained information that would find him guilty of one of his many crimes.

Catharine told Seth that when Jake was able to talk, the inspector spoke with him and Jake told him his story about how selfish he had been and how foolish. Jake told the inspector how well Grandfather had treated him and that he had paid him well, but he seemed to always want more. He asked the inspector to tell Grandfather that he was sorry, and he truly seemed to be sorry and that he was sad that he had repaid Grandfather's acts of kindness by being a traitor to everything he stood for.

Catharine said he even asked the inspector to apologize to her. But he said he knew when she came in and worked on Grandfather's books with him, that she would be able to discover in no time that the books had been tampered with. He said, women usually would not have understood the record keeping or the entries made in the books. But she did understand them, and he could tell that she would be able to immediately understand and clearly figure out the whole setup. This thought clearly led to his fatal mistake of trying to steal and do away with the tell-tale books.

William soon arrived with tea and he seemed to have an extra-special almost smile on his face this day. Catharine could not help but notice this because William's face was always unreadable. But not today!

Then William asked if he could do anything else for them, and they both looked at the small feast he had placed in front of them. Surely, they said, they had everything that they could ever wish for and they thanked him. William then turned to leave, and yes, that was a smile on his face, which by this time was not so unusual.

Catharine and Seth walked back into each other's arms once again and just thought about the comfort that they brought each other. Even in the midst of all that had happened, there was a joyful, peaceful feeling in their hearts. But then they decided they must let the others meet this new visitor.

Seth was in London. He was here all the way from America, all the way from North Carolina, and all the way from the Outer Banks. And on top of that, he had asked Catharine if she would marry him and she had said "yes!"

When they left the room they were so happy. It was impossible not to see that they loved each other and soon, when they could get their family matters settled, they would be planning a wedding. Of course, that would take place in the Outer Banks with families and friends of both Catharine and Seth in attendance. And, naturally, Father Sam would perform the ceremony which would be a special occasion for not only him, but their whole community.

Catharine couldn't keep these little thoughts from creeping into her mind... The beautiful sunshiny day, the little church cleaned and shining, all the people she had known and loved would be there. Even Anna Catharine would be there with Sarah and Abe. She would be the newest addition to the festivities. Then, they would have a wedding feast like none other in many a day because there would be wedding cake in addition to every delicious concoction known to these Bankers, and they knew some concoctions!

But, Catharine thought, I have to keep these thoughts to myself for a while. I will treasure them for just a little while in my own heart. Right now, I will introduce Seth to Grandfather Chase and Mrs. King.

Of course, Seth had always known Molly, but she surely would be surprised by this visit! And, it was Doctor Patrick's day to come by for Grandfather's regular checkup, so Seth would also meet Doctor Patrick. Catharine was so proud of Seth. She had never before seen him dressed in the latest men's fashions. She thought to herself that he surely had good taste because he was absolutely the most handsome man she had ever seen. But guess what, neither had Seth seen Catharine dressed in finery as she was today. And he too knew she, for sure, was the most beautiful girl on this earth.

CHAPTER 19

(The Introduction)

When they entered Grandfather's room, Catharine was almost speechless. She looked at Grandfather and then back to Seth. She said, "Grandfather, I would like for you to meet Seth Winters. Seth has surprised me beyond belief today. Seth, this is my Grandfather Chase. I am so happy for you to meet each other."

Grandfather was sitting in his favorite chair in his bedroom, which was now refurbished as a sitting room with comfortable chairs and accommodations for any guests he might have. Seth walked over to him with his hand stretched out. Seth said, "Mr. Chase, I feel like I know you. Catharine and her mother and father have told me so much about you. Some day soon I hope we can sit down and talk. I will tell you what I know about the Outer Banks if you will tell me about London?" Grandfather replied that he felt he already knew Seth also and that they would definitely have that talk.

He welcomed Seth to his home and told him he had only

to ask for anything he needed. Seth told him he was registered in a hotel not far away to which Grandfather Chase replied, "That most certainly will not do! We will have your things brought here immediately. We want you to be near to us so we can visit and get to know each other! Also, you know, we need to have that talk!" And so, that settled that!

Catharine introduced Seth to Mrs. King who immediately fell under his spell. Mrs. King said that he was a pleasant addition to this household and that he could not have come at a better time.

Seth was so glad to see Molly. When you are a long way from home, it is especially heartwarming to see a familiar and happy face. So Molly also received a bear hug from Seth. He told her he had brought Catharine and her gifts from home as well as messages. He said he declared that once people knew about his trip to England to visit them he was bombarded with requests to tell them this or tell them that. But he said, right now, suffice it to say, that I will give you the messages as I remember them because at this moment my mind is taking in too much information and I can hardly remember any of it! They all laughed at that because they knew exactly what he was talking about. They too were in that situation right now!

There was a soft knock at the door and William came in to say that Doctor Patrick was here to see Mr. Chase. Grandfather told William to send him in please and the introductions were made again for Doctor Patrick. Grandfather smiled and told Seth that he had some good news.

He told Seth that Doctor Patrick and Molly had just become engaged to be married! Seth was so gracious with his congratulations. Another handshake for Doctor Patrick and another hug for Molly. Then, Catharine said she also had news. Good news! Seth had come all the way to London on a mission. He had come to ask Catharine to marry him. And she had said "yes!" And the congratulations and hugs began to ring out again. In fact, Grandfather told them to put a stop to all of this for a few minutes. He said, "I am an old man and my heart can't stand all of these goings on at one time!"

It seemed the fog of the previous week's sadness had lifted. What a good feeling to have good news, celebrations, and happiness abounding again.

Catharine and Molly then excused themselves and left the men to their own devices. They used the moment to talk among themselves about the many happenings during the past few weeks. They couldn't believe that they were both engaged to be married and it all happened within a week's time. And another thing, they absolutely could not believe that Seth Winters was here in London! Nor that he came all this distance to ask for Catharine's hand in marriage. Now that is surely love!

The men talked a short while about Jake and how much his greediness had cost him, actually his whole life, and they talked of several more topics that interested them, but the conversation soon turned to life on the Outer Banks. They were all wanting to learn more about this place that seemed to tug at the heartstrings of everyone who heard about it.

As Seth talked you could tell that his heart was deeply imbedded there in those Outer Banks of North Carolina and it was with a great love that he spoke of it. He told of the warm, sunshiny weather. He talked of the people who lived there who were hardworking and caring. They shared all parts of their lives, the good and the bad, and they worked together for the common good. He told them that people there did not have a lot of money. They were not wealthy, but they were rich. When a baby was born they all celebrated and when a person died they all grieved.

He told them of the terrific storms in hurricane season and how they could be very devastating to the whole Atlantic seacoast. House windows were boarded up and any outside porch benches and chairs or any other items that these enormous winds could pick up with its great force were put in sheds or otherwise tied down to protect the neighborhood from flying debris. Also, he said people made sure they had several days worth of extra food, water and basic essentials on hand.

They would sometimes gather together in families' homes or other meeting places to wait out the storm. Believe it or not, he said, these were very special times for them. There was a bonding that took place in the face of possible danger that helped define these people. It was a time of sharing and caring.

During this time they retold many of the local folklore stories once again. And during those times, you can be sure one or two stories about the Black Pelican would be told. One of the newest of those favorite stories being the one where the Black Pelican brought attention to a certain ship needing assistance, and that was the ship bringing Catharine and her family to the Outer Banks.

Grandfather Chase and Doctor Patrick sat spellbound as Seth spun his stories. Seth's father was known on the "Banks" as the best of the storytellers. In fact, he could often be found on the porch of his warehouse where he kept his shipbuilding supplies spinning much loved stories. He also sold fishing supplies and the best seafood on the Banks. Everyone knew when you wanted the freshest fish for dinner, you went to John Winter's to buy them. His porch faced the ocean and while he was spinning his yarns and holding captive his audiences, the sea breezes and salty air set the stage automatically for him. It seemed to be a fact that Seth had inherited this lovable talent of storytelling from his father, which was such an important part of their heritage.

William came in just then to ask if Seth would like to go to the hotel and transfer his luggage, as his suite which was right next to Grandfather's was all ready. Doctor Patrick and Grandfather were so engrossed by the stories Seth was sharing with them that they hated to have them end but Grandfather at once invited Doctor Patrick to join them for dinner that night. He decided they could continue the stories then and so they were immediately looking forward to dinner. Seth seemed right at home with these men and they had found him to be someone they felt at ease with, someone you could trust and most certainly someone whose company you enjoyed.

Grandfather also asked Mrs. King to join them for dinner. Grandfather said he would have her picked up and driven home, so she needn't worry about that. She accepted readily because she had heard all of the stories thus far and, if she had a choice, she surely didn't want to miss anything. Besides, you could rest assured that when this group got together there were going to be points of interest discussed! At that time, and by that invitation alone, it was made known to her that she was no longer just an employee, but that she was a part of the family.

Seth then followed William and they left for the hotel to pick up Seth's belongings.

Seth shared with William that when he started his trip he had very little baggage, but he had felt (and had been instructed by his mother) that he needed to dress differently here. The simple clothing he wore on the Outer Banks was entirely different than the fancy clothing that young men wore in London-Town, so after the addition of his fine and fancy wardrobe, he had quite a collection. They both shared a laugh at this, but Seth added that he had to admit the feel of the fine cloth was not all that bad.

Seth was even more endeared to William by the fact that Seth shared these intimate details with him. Most wealthy and handsome young men of London would never discuss these types of private things with the butler!

It didn't take long for them to gather Seth's belongings from the hotel and soon they were heading back to Grandfather's home. William, who felt so at ease with Seth, was a great guide and told him the history of places of interest as they passed by and, of course, Seth was interested in everything.

When they arrived at the house, Catharine and Molly were visiting with Grandfather Chase. William and his staff carried Seth's baggage to his rooms and they were busy for a while getting things in order. Afterwards Seth rapped on Grandfather Chase's door to see if he wanted or needed any company but, obviously he needed neither. He was being entertained by two of the most beautiful ladies in the world, and when he told Grandfather this, Grandfather laughed and said he was in total agreement. They visited for a while and agreed they would all take a short rest before getting ready for a much looked forward to dinner.

The girls were already thinking about which dress they would wear to most impress their future husbands and which earrings and on and on.... They were so thankful that their home had changed from one of sickness and an unsettling atmosphere to one of uplifting thoughts and happy anticipation.

And when they met for dinner the men were outstanding in their finest. There was no doubt they wanted to impress the ladies as much as the ladies wanted to impress them. But it was hard to shine overmuch when those ladies were dressed in London's finest fashions. Every item had been chosen especially for them. Every color and every cut of every dress was fitted just to them and their choices had the desired effect on these men. They were lovely and very much appreciated for their beauty.

CHAPTER 20

(Excuse Me, But Don't I Know You?)

Then there came a knock at the door and William announced that Mrs. King had arrived. William again had a slight smile on his face as he ushered Mrs. King into the room (still very unusual for him). Immediately you knew why. They all had only seen Mrs. King in her nurse's uniform with no makeup or such, but this was an altogether different Mrs. King than they had seen. She was a beautiful middle aged lady dressed elegantly and stylishly. She wore a trace of makeup that just enhanced her natural beauty. They all "oohed and aahed" and it embarrassed her for a minute but then she smiled and thanked them graciously. Well, this was going to be some night....

Dinner was delicious as Grandfather had requested very special dishes to be prepared for his very special guests. This was truly a night of celebration in his home.

He welcomed all of them to dinner. Not only were there

two, but three beautiful ladies at his table. His beautiful grand-daughter, Catharine, and Molly, who he had grown to think of as a granddaughter too, and his nurse, Mrs. King, who had become much more than a nurse, but a dear family friend.

Then, he mentioned his beloved Doctor, Patrick, who had surely saved his life through his painstakingly careful care. Had Patrick not used all of the medical technology available to him Grandfather might not be sitting here with these very special people!

Finally, he welcomed Seth again, Grandfather was almost speechless. He was so thankful that Catharine had chosen such a man for her husband, and he was looking forward to hearing more stories from him about his homeland which they loved to hear.

Grandfather's health was so greatly improved. He felt better daily and was returning to life as he had known it before Jake had chosen his fateful path. The sadness that Jake had caused was still felt and they all were sad that they were powerless to help him, but they all knew they would have helped him if they had known how. With this in mind, they then decided the only choice they had was to move on with their lives.

"Now," Grandfather said, "I have something I want to ask all of you "Bankers!" He went on, "When Catharine's father, Thomas, was young, he took lessons on the violin. I believe he was considered to be a very good violinist. In fact he has been known to play for some rather large gatherings here in London. And now, I hear he plays a "fiddle"! Well, the laughter broke out with a thunderous roar and that is the way the entire evening went.

They laughed at times and they were entirely serious at times, but it was a very memorable evening. Mrs. King told a story or two from her family. Her husband had been an inspector for Scotland Yard and had lost his life in service to that department. So when Detective Casey was introduced on the case, she knew him and his comrades. She was well informed in such cases and knew what action she should take or should not take, and how to keep things to herself that needed to be kept quiet. In fact, she had even talked with the inspector several times when she had suspected Jake was acting suspiciously. So they all learned something new about each other that night.

As the night started to grow late though, Grandfather and Mrs. King bade the youngsters a goodnight and Grandfather walked with Mrs. King to the door. At the door, Grandfather asked Mrs. King if she had ever thought of taking a trip overseas? He told her that he had gotten so wrapped up in the stories of America and the Outer Banks that his curiosity had just gotten the best of him. She told him that she had always been a dreamer and that, of course, she wanted to see these far away places, especially when the people you met who lived there seemed to think of it as "heavenly"!

"Well", Grandfather said, "I am on the verge of just considering that trip. I want to see my son and his wife again. I want to see my granddaughter, Catharine, get married and maybe even see a grandchild. Do you think I am able to make the trip? Would you consider making the voyage with us. I would arrange for us to sail when Catharine and Seth and their party sails. Knowing you were there would make me feel more secure and I feel you would know how to deal with any emergency that would come up. Of course, I am feeling so well these days that I don't expect any, but it would be nice to know you were there." Grandfather told her to just think about it and they would talk more on it later.

When Mrs. King got home that night she had to sit for a while and gather her thoughts. She had never even thought seriously about leaving London before. Naturally, being the dreamer that she was, she yearned to see far off places, but to actually up and leave London! She just didn't know. Still, to be invited to join this family and sail into the unknown greatly appealed to her. She had enjoyed her time spent nursing Thomas Chase back to health. He was a very kind and uplifting patient and a person she believed that she would greatly miss if they were apart.

As she lay in bed, waiting for sleep to come, the idea seemed to become so much more right. She was still a young woman, only fifty years old. She had always been thrifty during her whole marriage, and she had a small inheritance, so she would be financially okay. And these people she had met, if the others were anything like them, she would learn to love in no time. In fact, they already seemed more like family than some people she had known all of her life in London. It is not really clear when this all happened, but it was apparent before sleep overtook her that night that her mind was made up.

If Thomas Chase wanted her to come to America, to this Outer Banks place with him to be his nurse, friend, or whatever, then she was going!

That night she dreamed of living by the sea in a little cottage. She felt the breeze blowing in through her window. She smelled the salt sea air and she even thought she saw the Black Pelican soaring in the sky above her. It was a dream of peace and of belonging with the love of family, who were remarkably not even her family. She slept so soundly, so undisturbed. How could she not know this was the right decision....

CHAPTER 21

(More Winds of Change)

The next morning Catharine's business sense clicked in and she knew she had to talk with Grandfather. They needed to discuss affairs regarding his many holdings and how they would best be handled. After she dressed for the day, she and Molly went to have breakfast as usual with Grandfather.

They talked about the grand time they had last night and they thanked him profusely for the elegant feast. The entire night was so enjoyed by all. They especially enjoyed the part about the "fiddle," at which they all laughed again, but Catharine told him that if he could hear her Dad play that fiddle, he would immediately know the difference! He said, I am sure I would.

Then she said she would like to talk with him after breakfast regarding the business and how best different aspects should be handled. She wanted all of his ideas. It was so good to see his mind sharp again. She knew he would help her with sensible advice and that he was now up to the task.

That morning Seth had arranged to meet with his ship-building acquaintances and spend the day going over the differences in the way they plied their trades. They believed each of them had ideas that could be beneficial to the other's business. This gave Grandfather and Catharine a perfect time to examine certain legal and business areas needing their immediate attention.

They poured over the books, as she had done with Mr. Spencer and Jake. They found missing parts, as they knew they would. They talked over certain things and they both agreed some things could be improved upon. And, more importantly, they knew that neither of them wanted to constantly deal with this huge group of all-consuming responsibilities!

They then agreed, after a lot of discussion that they needed to turn the whole matter over to a group of professionals that they could rely upon.

Grandfather immediately suggested that they consider the firm of his old friend, Mr. Spencer, whose son had taken over the business now that his father had retired. Catharine, who had taken a liking to Mr. Spencer from day one, agreed that this was a great choice, one that they both would be comfortable with. Confident that they had made the right choice they were much relieved. Now they were getting somewhere!

They contacted the company that afternoon and the next

day they had set up meetings. The changeover was beginning.

Catharine was feeling so relieved to have someone both she and Grandfather trusted to be in charge of business decisions from now on. They worked for the rest of the week getting books to balance and making final decision about many things. Finally, they were satisfied that they had done all they could possibly do to get everything in order for the new managers of Grandfather's estate. It was a decision that allowed them to breathe easier as they knew that the company was an ethical one that they could always trust! They even proceeded to remove all of the books from Grandfather's office to their new location.

Catharine would no longer need to have the responsibility of an empire on her hands or on her mind. The business was now in efficient, able, and ethical hands. You might say, it had been a good day's work!

Grandfather and Catharine talked after the meeting was over. He told her that he always hated putting all of that weight on her shoulders, but that he wanted her to inherit everything he had. He told her that he wanted her to use it in its entirety to do whatever she wanted, and said he knew that with her heart and sharp mind he would approve of any choices she would make.

Then they parted until the dinner hour, satisfied with decisions they had made and that throughout the many changes and negotiations, they had been in complete agreement.

At dinner that night, at which Doctor Patrick was also present again, they talked of their decision that day to relinquish all business decisions to Mr. Spencer's company, now being overseen by his son. They seemed completely at ease with their decision, which was certainly a relief to all.

Soon the conversation took a different turn and Grandfather told them of his conversation with Mrs. King the night before. He told them, "I'll bet you all will never guess what I discussed with Mrs. King last night before she left? I asked her, if I could arrange it, and if you all agree that I am able, if she would be willing to sail with us to the Outer Banks! I want to see my son and his wife again. I want to be with my granddaughter and her husband and see where they live. I want to get to meet my grandsons and granddaughters when they arrive."

"Do you think I am making a mistake by wanting to do this at my age? It is not a mistake, I can assure you! I have spent my whole life without the companionship of my family. Oh, they lived in London with me, but I never enjoyed the pleasures that they could have brought... until now. It took an event that almost took my life to make me see that. I guess, sadly, I can thank Jake for bringing it to my attention. Now I have decided I want to spend my days, however many that may be, close to my son and his wife and my granddaughter and Seth."

Well, this morning when Mrs. King arrived she wholeheartedly agreed to accompany us on our journey. This makes me happy because she and I have become great friends, and maybe even more! She is a wonderful, caring nurse and a heck of a chess player. I look forward to many a good chess game with her while we are on our way to America.

Catharine broke out and just literally bawled at this! She was so happy. She could not control her tears nor the joy these words brought. She ran over to her Grandfather's chair and clasped her arms around his shoulders and told him he had made her the happiest girl in the world! Then she was joined by Molly and another outburst followed. "Okay, Okay", Grandfather replied. "So I take it that you agree I can come and visit your American home? I will start making arrangements right now!"

"Hold on," Doctor Patrick said. "I don't think you should go anywhere without your doctor present. After all, we have been inseparable for a long time!"

"Well Patrick," says Grandfather, "Since I feel so much better now, I didn't know you would object to my making this trip. However, if you know of some reason I shouldn't go, please let me know and I will reconsider."

Doctor Patrick says, "Well I certainly will let you know of one reason for you to reconsider and that is that you can only go if I can go with you."

"Wait one minute," Seth says. "This is becoming confusing. Did I hear correctly that all of us will be returning to the Outer Banks. Even Mrs. King? Patrick, did I hear that right?"

"You did," said Patrick. "Molly and I have agreed that we want to be a part of that new settlement in the Outer Banks. Her family is there, which naturally suggests that she would like to live there. But, more importantly, we both feel it is the right place for us to live and raise our children. We want them to be raised in an atmosphere where they can roam and play as they will. As I hear you all talk of this place, I also believe this is the perfect place for me to practice medicine. So, when the boat sails, Molly and I will be on board also, with our hopes and plans for the future laid right on the line with yours."

"Also, we will be planning a wedding there. We want her parents and her friends and loved ones to attend. Do you think there will be enough room on the ship, or for that matter, on the Outer Banks for all of us? I hope so."

Catharine and Molly danced around like children. They had always been so close and Catharine once had feared that Molly and Patrick would stay in London when they sailed for home. Now the thought occurred to both of them that just maybe they could plan a double wedding? What would the families think about that? What would the guys think about that? Well, they had plenty of time to plan for that. They had so much to think about right now that they didn't need to add one more thing to this boiling pot!

It seemed that everything was coming together and that possibly it wouldn't be long until they would all be sailing to America. It was unbelievable the changes that had occurred in the past few days.

In fact ever since Seth arrived. Had he been responsible in some way for pushing them all into making these decisions? You know, it didn't hurt a thing because he was a natural born leader. He knew how to get things done and he certainly wasn't one to sit back and wait for others to get the ball rolling. He was just what they all needed right now.

CHAPTER 22

(The Plan)

Seth suggested that they all make lists of what they each needed to do in preparation for their trip. Then, every day until they sailed, they would meet and discuss how best to accomplish them. Since there were at last count six people who would be sailing together, there would be different requirements needed for each of them.

So they all split up to begin their lists and they all worked like a team together to make everything go as smoothly as possible. And, guess what, when they got together for their meeting the next day, it was apparent that each one had taken their task of list-making seriously. In fact, they all had already crossed off some of the items from their lists. They all said they had worked late into the night trying to think of any little thing they might have missed.

Of course, Grandfather had the largest and most complicated list. And as Mrs. King had the least complicated list, she proved her worth immediately by painstakingly helping tend to Mr. Chase's list. In fact, he was one of the first to state proudly that his list was completed.

Grandfather called William aside and they talked about the keeping of the house and grounds. He left William in complete control of the house, grounds and the staff. He had set up an account at his bank and William was to use it at his discretion for salaries, repairs, weekly expenses like food. And the list went on. He also made William a wealthy man by opening an account for him in an amount that totally shocked William. However, Grandfather Chase told him he was *never* to use this money for household expenses, ever! This was his personal account to be used as he saw fit. He even told William that he might use some of it to sail to America one day? To which William responded, "After the changes occurring here this week, nothing would surprise me!"

But, first and foremost Mr. Chase wanted William to know that he alone was in charge of the house and grounds. In return, Mr. Chase rewarded him handsomely, more than William had ever dreamed of earning, in addition to the generous account he opened for him. He asked him if he and his wife would possibly be willing to move into one of the apartments in the house. Mr. Chase would feel more comfortable knowing someone he trusted was in the house at all times. William said he felt he would be able to make all of this come about.

Mr. Chase also told William that Mr. Spencer would be

checking in with him from time to time to see if he needed anything and he also added that William should feel free to use the funds set aside with Mr. Spencer for his use, in fact, Grandfather said he would be checking to see that William did just that. When William saw a need, he should always feel entirely free to call on Mr. Spencer's firm when expenses happened to come up, for anything large or small, or even just to ask a question.

William said he felt comfortable with the arrangements. He had known Mr. Spencer for many years and knew he would be able to trust his advice, if he should ever need it.

But William had to chuckle under his breath, "I don't believe I have ever been told that I *must* spend freely, or that I will be checked on to *make sure* that I spend freely!".... But, I believe I will be able to adjust.

THE BLACK PELICAN

PART VI

CHAPTER 23

(Making the Plan Work)

Those nights around the dinner table proved to be some of the happiest times of Grandfather Chase's life. He, at last, felt a camaraderie with his family that he had never experienced before. He felt he was at long last a vital and important part of the discussions they were having and the decisions they were making. Until now, he had felt like he was the one who wielded the power over most decision making but he now realized it was not him but his money that had given him so much power.

How liberating it felt knowing his opinions were important to them because he was now a part of the process. They were all working *together*, which was something he had not been used to doing. His opinion had, until now, been the final one. Strange how this seemingly loss of power seemed to empower him!

Mrs. King was now a nightly visitor at their table. As a group, they all felt responsible for helping to see that her list was completed also.

She had one item that was of considerable concern to her. She owned her little cottage and it held very special memories for her. She and her husband had made this special purchase when they were married and they had lived there together from the day they were married until his death. They had shared everything together and though they were never blessed with children, she always felt blessed because of the love they shared and they were blessed with careers which gave them a great sense of purpose, she as a nurse and he as a detective for Scotland Yard. He had worked together with Detective Casey for many years before his death and Detective Casey had been a helpful and faithful friend to her since her husband's death.

Now, though she was preparing to leave her little cottage for a land which was totally strange to her, and though she looked forward to the adventure with great anticipation, her heart was heavy when she thought of leaving this cottage which she loved so well. She was deep in thought when there came a knock at her front door.

When she answered the door Doctor Patrick and the young nurse who had sat with Grandfather Chase at night were standing there smiling while a pouring rain pounded down on them. Mrs. King hurriedly ushered them in, laughed and asked them if they were lost out here on this dreary, rainy day.

As it turned out, they were not lost at all. It seems the young nurse was newly engaged to be married and she and her husband-to-be were searching for a small property to buy. She and Doctor

Patrick had been talking earlier in the day at the hospital and she had mentioned that they were in the market to buy a small cottage. Of course, Dr. Patrick immediately thought of Mrs. King's cottage. She had visited with Mrs. King several times and they had developed a close friendship, so she knew the cottage well and it suited their needs perfectly.

This was just the solution Mrs. King needed. She would be much happier leaving here knowing that the new owners would appreciate this little home as much as she had. As they talked about the financial aspects of buying the home, they both felt a deal was near to being made.

Mrs. King told her that she would love to leave the furniture and everything else in the house as a part of the sale. The only thing she would remove from the house would be her personal things. This news delighted this young bride because, as with so many newly married couples, the expense of buying and furnishing a home is frightening. Mrs. King told her that she was so pleased to have someone like her buy her home that these things would just be included in the price of the house.

Mrs. King then took them out into her English flower and vegetable garden. Of this she was particularly proud and always tended it with loving care. Since she had no children to take up her spare time, she devoted many hours of her days here. And it showed! It was lovely and in it were beautiful and unusual flowers and plants.

Mrs. King also loved to cook and had a large collection of old family recipes that were tried and true. She noted that she must remember to pack these. Then when they had one of those get-togethers that Catharine and Seth had talked about, she would surely be able to pull out a delicious recipe of her very own to share with everybody. Maybe a dish much different from any they had ever tasted before! Another new adventure....

When they left, she asked Mrs. King if she could bring her future husband by that evening to see the house, to which Mrs. King readily agreed. Another job well done, Doctor Patrick! And Mrs. King's list was immediately completed....

Their lists were reviewed and it appeared that they were all ready to begin their much awaited trip. They spent some time going over the details and were all satisfied that they couldn't think of a thing that they had left undone.

Then they all relaxed and enjoyed their dinner. This would be one of the few meals they would have left to eat around Grand-father's bountiful table together. Even though they were all look-ing forward to their new adventures on the Outer Banks of North Carolina, the thought of these life-changing events made them all a little sad too.

Seth then, sensing the need for a lighter topic, asked if anyone there had heard of two brothers from Ohio who were working to develop a flying machine. They had been toying with this idea for awhile and had a lot of people excited about the possibility. Some viewed this as a wildly outrageous crazy scheme, but the more forward-thinking viewed this as a glimpse into the future where man could soar with the birds in the clouds with unlimited freedom. While looking for the ideal place to test their machine and to improve its performance, they discovered that the steady winds of the Outer Banks provided the perfect setting for the testing of their very primitive flying machine.

They talk of the day when men would actually fly inside of one of these machines, and maybe they would eventually even cross the ocean! Can you imagine that! There are tall sand dunes in the Outer Banks and in one area in Kill Devil Hills, there is an area with especially tall dunes. This is the spot where they have chosen to do their testing because they need the steady winds which are common to that area to help lift their machines into the air.

Grandfather Chase was very interested in this topic. He said he had no doubt that one day because of what these two men so strongly believed in, that there would be men flying in one of these machines. After all, he said, look at the latest thing, the automobile. Surely there were naysayers back in the day saying this was not going to happen, but it has, and the automobile will continue to grow and improve its performance. And also, electricity. Just in its infancy, I believe. How about the telegraph. As it is perfected, it will change the world. That is the way I see it.

The entire dinner table applauded at this point. What a speech of optimism. Grandfather Chase knew what dreamers were made of.

Then, with a voice that bespoke great pride he said he learned that lesson from his son. He told how his son was a dreamer who had left the security of a life of ease and embarked on a life in which he could follow his own dreams. He had not taken the easy road, but the road that he felt would make a difference in his life, his family's life and maybe help bring about a change for the betterment of his entire new homeland. And hadn't he done that? Hadn't he brought many changes to his new homeland that had made life easier for his fellow Bankers. Yes, Grandfather Chase himself had *learned* what dreamers were made of, and he had learned it from his son!

The tears which were running down Catharine's cheeks were tears of pride. She had never been as proud of her Grandfather as when he shared these feelings about her father with them.

Catharine then asked Molly if she had replied to her father about the possibility of a dress shop in part of his new addition to his store complex. Molly said she had and had also written to several ladies who had helped her in the past when her workload was too heavy (such as when they were making clothes for Catharine's trip to England). She had asked them if they would consider working for her in her shop if she should decide to open the shop. She said she had not had responses from them as yet, but felt sure that there was a good possibility that they would help her in the shop. She also said she was going shopping the next day for two new sewing machines, which she knew she would need. Also, she would be shopping for many odds and ends she would need for this new undertaking.

Catharine then asked if she could go along. She also told Molly that one of her friends owned one of the better shops in London and if Molly wanted to, they could stop by her shop. Catharine felt she could surely give them some good tips as to what she would need to start up her shop, and also some good tips as to what she may not want to keep in stock. Too, Catharine added, possibly she would be able to help her find reputable suppliers that she could depend on to make shipments to her as she needed them. Molly said she had so many questions already in her mind that it would be so helpful to her to have someone knowledgeable to help her.

The next morning the girls were up early. They were happy, as ladies always are, to know they were going shopping! Also, Seth and Patrick were accompanying them, so in the middle of the day there would be a luncheon, which would be left up to the guys to oversee. In the meantime, they both would be busy trying to learn as much as possible about opening a lady's boutique in the Banks.

Catharine's friend, Maria, was a lady who was prepared with a plan in hand. Immediately Molly could see why her business in London was such a success. She had made a list of possible suppliers, what items they sold that Molly would most likely need, their addresses, and she also said she would be in contact with them all to let them know about Molly and about her new venture in America. She helped Molly also by recommending companies who sold sewing machines and their parts. Molly knew she would need to buy several sewing machines today, and in the future she would need a reliable company to replace worn and broken parts as well as new machines.

Maria also recommended several new fabric suppliers, and even the best thread on the market. She showed Molly her display windows and supplied her with many ideas to take home for her own window dressings. There were some items Maria talked with Molly about that they laughed about though. Molly told Maria that corsets and silk stockings, high-heeled shoes and those types of things were not particularly in demand on the Banks, but she would try a sampling because you never knew what the vacationers might try! Also, the women of the Banks would get a laugh thinking of themselves attired as such!

Then they told Maria their exciting news. They told her they were both engaged to be married to two wonderful men. Molly told her first of her fairy tale story of meeting Doctor Patrick Kelly. That he was Grandfather Chase's doctor and they had fallen in love immediately. She told her that they would be married in America and Patrick would start his new medical practice there. She told Maria that her parents were so excited to meet Patrick and that she knew they would love him. His Irish ancestry was such a good fit for their family because her dad and Patrick both had inherited so many of the same characteristics.

Then Catharine told Maria her love story of the "boy back home" in America who showed up on her Grandfather's doorstep one morning after receiving her letter saying that she was overwhelmed by the decisions she was having to make. She couldn't believe her eyes when she saw him there! He told her that when he returned to America, it would only be if she was with him. He asked her to marry him right there and said he had already gotten her Mother and Father's approval. And he told her that he would be there with her helping her with any decisions she ever had to make from that day forward! And, of course, I said "Yes!"

Next they asked Maria if they could come back in several days to look at fabrics suitable for wedding dresses. They would need all the accessories and fabrics for their Mothers' dresses also, and they would have to make a list of other items they would need. They told Maria, however, that these weddings would not be like London weddings, but much simpler. However, they still wanted them to be elegant.

Maria's eyes were flashing. You could see her brain was working a mile a minute. She got it....

When they left Maria, Molly knew she had found a life-long friend and business contact who would prove to be irreplaceable over the years. To have such a successful businesswoman in London as a friend and confidante was without price. Molly collected her lists prepared by Maria, the addresses, and pages of many suggestions. There were so many that Maria knew Molly wouldn't be able to remember them all, so she wrote them down. But she told Molly that as things developed and as she remembered things she had not listed she would write them down and send them to her. They left the shop knowing that they had collected first-class, first-hand suggestions that would be invaluable.

It was then that they both realized they were starving! The guys had been wandering around the shops in the neighborhood while the ladies had talked and shopped at their leisure. Molly and Catharine were just leaving Maria's shop when they spotted them coming toward them. They were both hugging their stomachs and complaining of severe hunger pains and the fact that they were being cruelly starved, to which the girls replied: "But we have much more shopping to do yet! We can't possibly stop now!" The guys thought they were serious and then they said they really did feel the hunger pains! The girls gave in and said, "Let's go eat." This was so what they wanted to hear and little did they know the girls were as hungry as they were.

Patrick suggested a small French restaurant which was a favorite of his. He said they needed to take advantage of the dining diversities because he didn't know how many French restaurants he would find in the Outer Banks. Molly replied saying, "At the rate our sailing party is increasing, don't mention it or we could possibly be sailing with the addition of the resident French chef added to the mix!"

After a delicious lunch, they were all rejuvenated and mentally and physically prepared to take on the shopping for the remaining items for Molly's shop. After several hours they were headed back to Grandfather Chase's having bought the sewing machines, fabrics, threads, buttons, and the many miscellaneous items needed for the newest clothing shop soon to be introduced in the Outer Banks.

Now, what would be a good name for such a business....

One thing agreed on by all was that each one still wanted to purchase gifts for those back home. So the next day was filled with this important project. Of course, Mrs. King's gifts were ideal to ship because they would take up very little space and because they were lightweight. She was excited because her gifts of flower and vegetable seeds would produce much interest from the local gardeners as to how each one would grow there compared to how they grew in London. She may even have packed some flower and vegetable seeds that would be new to them. They had all agreed to try and keep the items small and lightweight which would help tremendously with the shipping and the handling of so many items. They did a good job of adhering to this rule, with only a few exceptions.

They bought trinkets the likes not found in the Banks, they bought material for new dresses for the mothers, they put much thought into what they bought each person, but the one they had the most fun buying for was Anna Catharine! This is where the rule that the items be small and lightweight was broken. There were large stuffed animals, the newest in baby toys and clothes. What was so funny is that they each broke this same rule. They all broke the rule when shopping for Anna Catharine!

Grandfather Chase and Catharine had gone through the house and selected articles of furniture, portraits and other things that they knew her mother and father would like to have. These things would be shipped at a later date. Of course, if there were additional items that they wanted, they had only to let William and Mr. Spencer know and they would have them shipped later also.

So now the only thing the girls had left to do was to visit Maria's shop and pick out the fabrics for their gowns and the accessories, and possibly the accessories for their mother's outfits. Maria's area of expertise was so helpful. It was as if she automatically knew what fabrics and styles would work on the island. She said that she could have the dresses made and shipped to them when they were finished, however they both agreed, they wanted to buy the fabric and accessories, but they wanted Molly to be the seamstress. Catharine and Molly soon made their decisions. They had talked among themselves so much about the dresses and styles that they already knew what they wanted. After the decisions were made, Maria told them she would have their order delivered to Mr. Chase's home later in the day.

CHAPTER 24

(The Departure)

So the time had come for their journey to begin. That night, the final night before they sailed for America, Grandfather Chase had arranged a farewell dinner with himself, Catharine, Seth, Doctor Patrick, Molly and Mrs. King as hosts and the guests would be his entire household staff. He set aside this night especially to honor those faithful people who had been like his family for many years. He gave very generous gifts to all and all who wished would be in his employ until they retired or had reason to leave, at which time they would be taken care of for the rest of their lives. He told them he hoped to see them all again. Grandfather Chase told them they all would hold a special place in his heart and he would never forget their faithful service to him. Then they all wined and dined as if all were royalty. They may not truly be royalty, but Mr. Chase had made each of them very well off!

As they said their goodnights that night, there were many tears on many cheeks, I'll tell you! Such a night is truly bittersweet...

The next morning saw everybody up at an early hour. They were to be at the ship prepared to board at seven a.m. Their belongings had been loaded the day before and the only things they carried were very small personal items, which made the process of boarding much simpler. They had an early breakfast at Grandfather's home and the cook had packed them all snacks and, as they all laughed and said, she had packed enough food for the entire trip!

They were a handsome group heading toward America. All of them were as well prepared as was possible for the trip. It had been such a smart decision on the part of Seth for them all to make their lists, and also to help with the lists of those whose situations were more complicated. Mrs. King was especially grateful to Doctor Patrick who was responsible for instigating the sale of her home. He had solved a problem that could have been huge for her.

Mrs. King had something else of great importance on her mind. Doctor Patrick had asked her if she would be interested in being his nurse when he set up his new office in the Banks. He indicated that Mr. Chase didn't need much medical attention these days and he said it would provide opportunities for them both to meet the locals much sooner and get to know their habits and traditions first hand.

Mrs. King was so thankful again to Doctor Patrick for thinking of her. That was the only thing that worried her. She knew that Mr. Chase was less needy now and the thought had crossed her mind that she was entering this new life unlike any of the others. She had no kin, and until now she had nothing of value to offer. That was, until now....

The ship was docked and their little group was being escorted out to meet it. Grandfather and Mrs. King led the way, giving special attention to Grandfather as he slowly and carefully planted each foot. Even though he had gained much ground health wise, he was still not as surefooted or strong as he would like to be, but he made out well. Then he was there to encourage and help Mrs. King each step of the way.

She was more steady on her feet, but it was quite a pull for her also. Always the caretaker and never the one to be taken care of, she told him not to worry, She was saving her energies to beat him at chess when they got settled down. Little did she know that when they got settled down, both of them would immediately have to take a little nap! And now the Doctor and Molly boarded and lastly Catharine and her Seth. What would she have done without her Seth!

They were all shown at once to their rooms which would be home to them for the trip across the Atlantic. Their luggage had already been deposited in each of their rooms.

The day was clear and warm, which was unusual for a late fall day in London. Catharine, Molly and Mrs. King went with

Grandfather Chase to his quarters to be sure that everything was in order for him. It was. His luggage had been deposited and was already being unpacked and neatly put away in his closet and chests of drawers. They made sure that he knew where each thing he needed could be located then they left him to see to caring for the needs of their own personal belongings.

Their rooms were much different than their rooms at Grandfather Chase's lovely home, but they were clean and comfortable. They were small and cozy and well appreciated by all. They were all pretty much the same, with dark mahogany walls with the needed furniture only; a bed, dresser, chest of drawers, a chair and a small desk for writing. But, what else would they need until they reached their destination. Only the necessities were provided when you were at sea.

That evening they had a delicious dinner with the captain. He explained that they probably would not experience this type of dinner every night, but they had come a long way and had learned a lot about the preparation of their foods and how to preserve them and make them more tasty. They enjoyed the company of other passengers for a while and soon they all said goodnight.

It had been a long day for everyone....

The next morning everybody woke early. There were the noises made by the crew which were strange to all of them. They were hungry for breakfast and were delighted when they were served a delicious one. Grandfather said he had slept like a log and Mrs. King said she had also. Of course, the younger set had slept soundly. Now what to do to fill the day. Mrs. King said she would be interested in a long chess game. Grandfather agreed to be her partner. The girls had brought books to read, and that left Patrick and Seth free to visit with the hands on board and collect some more tales to tell around the campfires in the days and years ahead.

That night they enjoyed another tasty dinner and afterwards they all gathered in Grandfather's room and talked and talked. Seth was, as usual, up for a tale or two. Tonight he shared the story of the Lost Colony. The story of Virginia Dare, the first English child born in America. Another favorite story told around many a table or bonfire in the Outer Banks. Virginia Dare's father left Roanoke Island, as one of the stories go, to return to England for supplies. When he returned several years later, the whole colony had disappeared. Many theories abounded as to what happened to them, but none have ever been proven. Seth, of course, had his own opinion, that they had tried to return to England and had gotten lost at sea, but that too has never been proven. He shared some of the many stories of Blackbeard, the pirate, which always pleased. These were of special interest to Patrick who was mesmerized by Seth's storytelling and his realistic accounts of each tale.

Catharine sat close at Seth's side. She was so in love with this man who actually took her breath away that sometimes she caught herself just staring at him. He was so very handsome but he possessed so many qualities that she loved that his handsomeness was secondary.

She thought about the night that she knew she loved him. How he seemed to always care for everyone else before he thought of himself. How he helped the oldest to their seats. How he made sure they had their plates filled. How he made sure his mother and the other ladies who had cooked and were serving the delicious meal needed no help. How he even checked on his sister who was expecting her baby soon. He needed to know she was comfortable before he prepared his plate to eat. He was a gentleman inside and out and he was going to be her husband! How did she survive before she knew she loved Seth. Since discovering that she loved him, her life had taken on a totally different meaning. A peace, for which she was so thankful....

During the journey home the little group of six talked about the different areas of their lives and each came to know the other on a different level.

They found that Molly was not a good sailor. When the sea was calm she managed to feel only sort-of-okay, but when the waves tossed their little ship during storms at sea, she had to withdraw from the group and lay down on her bed where she tried not to move a muscle so that her head and stomach would calm down.

Doctor Patrick gave her a medication for seasickness which helped some, but until the weather calmed, she continued to stay in her bed. Catharine and Mrs. King would creep in her room and check on her often but if she were asleep they would creep back out without her even knowing they had been there. They felt that rest would be the best thing for her until the storms passed. Thankfully, the weather was calming this evening, the boat was riding smoothly on the sea, and Molly was beginning to gain ground.

The others didn't seem to be affected by the rolling movements and rising and falling of the ship. Catharine felt that, if Molly had her way, when she reached the shores of home it would be very unlikely that she would ever set foot off dry land again. She shared this thought with Molly later and Molly laughed and totally agreed with her. Catharine was relieved that she traveled well by ship because she felt that she would need to travel to London occasionally during her lifetime. She knew she would want to be there when any unusual decisions had to be made regarding her Grandfather's (which was now hers) estate.

Seth also had shown an interest in the shipbuilding techniques that he had learned of while in London, and there were many which had peaked his interest. With this new interest uncovered, Catharine felt Seth would be making business trips on occasion also. Seth had invited the owner of the company he had visited in London to visit his company in America and his invitation had been accepted. He was very proud of his and his father's accomplishments and was anxious to show off some of their achievements in return.

CHAPTER 25

(Journey's End)

That evening they were told the ship was drawing closer to shore and their journey was nearing an end. They talked of preparing their luggage for unloading. They had unpacked as little as possible in order to make the transition easier when they arrived in port.

The captain told them at dinner that they could expect to see land the next day and asked them to prepare as best they could for their arrival in America. He spoke to Grandfather Chase, Mrs. King and Patrick then, and with a very heartfelt voice welcomed them to America. He said he was confident that by the next time his ship came into port they would be wholehearted "Bankers." I say that, he said, because the people there are unique and caring, and are concerned with the simpler more important things of life. One day soon, I am going to retire and I will return here to stay. So I hope you enjoy your new life here and keep an eye out because one of these days before long I will be joining you! They all clapped their hands at this and assured him that they would be waiting.

Their families on the Outer Banks were as excited as the ones arriving. There had been much preparation for these six people.

Catharine would, of course, stay at home, in her own room, just a skip from her beloved seashore. Her Grandfather would, for now, stay with Catharine and her mother and father in their guest room. Grandfather had already made known that he wanted a small cottage of his own near his son and his family. This was totally expected because they all knew he would want to be independent and on his own, but close to his family.

Catharine's mother had arranged for Mrs. King to room and board with a widowed lady who usually catered to the summer visitors. This would just fill the bill for Mrs. King, until she could find her own place. They would most likely enjoy each other's company as Mrs. Miller was English also and had come here many years ago with her husband who had died several years ago.

Molly would also, of course, be staying at home with her parents. She was so excited and looking forward to them meeting her new husband-to-be. She knew they would adore Patrick and he them. The hours just could not pass fast enough for her. She had missed them so. Patrick was going to stay with Seth's family until he could locate the just-right home. Seth's family had graciously invited Patrick to use their spare bedroom as long as was needed. His plan was for he and Molly to find a home that they could move into after their wedding, or maybe they would have to build a new one, they just didn't know yet.

That left Seth, who would go home to the only home he had ever known. His mother had been cleaning and cooking for a week getting things in order for Seth and also for their special guest, Doctor Patrick. Seth couldn't wait for the folks to meet Patrick. They would love his happy and outgoing personality. He was a natural-born Banker!

Furthermore this is the week of Thanksgiving! A favorite time of year for them all every year, but this year seemed even more special. First of all, there would be thanks given for Anna Catharine. Everyone on the ship could not wait to see her! They would give thanks for Grandfather and his miraculous recovery and his new life here with his family who had missed him so. Then, there was going to be a new nurse on the island and the women especially couldn't wait to talk with her about the new vegetable and flower seeds she was bringing and also there were the new recipes. Who ever met a woman who didn't enjoy sitting together and talking with each other about those things. Also, they were all interested in the relationship that seemed to be blossoming between Mrs. King and Grandfather Chase....

Then they would give thanks for not one, but two upcoming weddings. They would give thanks for Molly and Patrick. They would be thankful that they found each other in a big city like London, and they would be thankful to have a much-needed new doctor on the island.

And with happy hearts they would give thanks for Catharine and Seth and their upcoming marriage. Not one person would forget Seth's immediate decision to go to London when he learned that Catharine needed him (and she had even told him so!) And the list would go on and on. The prayer of thanks around the table this Thanksgiving would take a while!

After they had gotten to their rooms that evening, they each packed every single thing that would not be used before they reached shore. This was a well-organized group and with Seth making sure they each had everything they needed and making sure he couldn't do anything more, he too headed toward his cabin. But something caught his eye as he looked out over the ship....

The moon was bright as day and the water was smooth. Was that Catharine? He walked over to her and spoke softly to get her attention. He was afraid he would startle her. As she turned around, he put his arms out and she was instantly in them. Then, he kissed her. She had never experienced a kiss like this. Nor had she experienced a feeling like this. Then, without saying a word, Seth turned her toward her cabin, walked with her there, kissed her softly again, and left her. It's a good thing he didn't say anything that required an answer, because she was speechless!

They retired early that night because they knew the wake-up call could possibly come early in the morning, but they had done all that could be done. And yes, the wakeup call came early the next morning. The captain asked everyone to gather for an early breakfast and after that the excitement really began.

They donned their hats and jackets. The air was chilly this

morning. They said goodbye to their rooms, which had served them well during the trip. They checked every nook and cranny there and then they closed the door and walked out to face their future.

As they drew near the shore they could see people gathered. Their little group of six stood tightly together straining to see something or someone they recognized. Slowly they started to wave in recognition. Slowly they waved and slowly the waves started to grow stronger until they could hear voices, then they could hear the voices singing "Welcome Home!" The whole community had gathered. They were singing together. And do you know what...

As they looked skyward, they saw it. A welcome like none other. Swooping and soaring there and leading the way to shore sailed that great beacon of hope of the Outer Banks,

The Beloved Black Pelican!

THE BELOVED BLACK PELICAN

The evening was dark and storm clouds rolled.
Winds blew and howled as rain beat and poured.

But one look skyward as that dark storm did blow,
Caused fears to subside, gave hearts new hope.

A magnificent bird, renowned for his valor,
Would gallantly, fearlessly lead them ashore.

C. T. Brookman

THE LEGEND OF THE BLACK PELICAN

If you are fortunate enough to visit the Outer Banks of North Carolina, a copy of the "Legend of the Black Pelican" is available to all customers of the outstanding BLACK PELICAN restaurant in Kitty Hawk, North Carolina. The restaurant is said to be incorporated into the original Kitty Hawk Lifesaving Station referred to in my story.

www.ingramcontent.com/pod-product-compliance
Lightning Source LLC
Chambersburg PA
CBHW060944180626
46817CB00004B/1709